Manifesting and Mischief

Beth Dolgner

Manifesting and Mischief
Crones of a Feather Paranormal Cozy Mysteries, Book Three

Ebook ISBN-13: 978-1-958587-44-7
Print ISBN-13: 978-1-958587-45-4

Published by Redglare Press

Cover Design: Melody Simmons

https://bethdolgner.com

CONTENTS

CHAPTER ONE

"IS THAT WHAT I think it is?"

The woman's mouth was slowly moving in an expression that was neither a smile nor a frown. There was no way for me to tell if she was delighted or disgusted.

"I assure you, I cleaned and disinfected it," I said quickly. "I needed a handcart, but this was sitting around, and it seemed like a good—"

The woman squealed as she brought the palms of both hands together. "I love it! Wait! I have to get photos of my products on there!"

I felt my entire body sag with relief. My regular customers were already used to the old stainless steel gurney I'd pressed into service as a cart to get deliveries into and out of the back of my vintage black hearse. I'd been using the gurney for about a month, and it was making life as the owner of Dead Easy Delivery a lot more convenient for me. Still, whenever I worked with a new client, I worried they would be horrified at having their goods shuttled around on the same gurney that had once wheeled dead bodies into a funeral home.

The owner of the local kitchenware shop chatted happily as she snapped photo after photo. I was happy to wait, though I had to ignore the frigid wind that was whipping against my cheeks. Finally, she wrapped up and gestured toward the back of the hearse. "I'm all done. It's too cold to be out here for long without a coat."

I lifted my hands, waggling my fingers and showing off my black wool gloves. "That's the one downside of this gurney. That stainless steel gets cold!" I opened the back door of the hearse, then pushed one end of the gurney against the bumper. The wheeled legs automatically folded up, and the whole thing slid inside the hearse easily, my client's packages on top of it.

The built-in rollers in the back of the Cadillac hearse made loading up easier, too, and they were one of my favorite things about using such an unlikely vehicle for my delivery service.

The attention I got—and the business that stemmed from it—was my other favorite thing about the hearse.

I said goodbye to my newest client, then headed to the post office with her packages. She had explained that her store received a lot of online orders, but it was tough for her to get away long enough to mail them out. I was more than happy to fill that gap for her.

There was a relatively short line at the post office, which I was grateful for. When I moved out of the magical town of Foxfire Haven, Washington, at the age of eighteen, I had realized the post office in my hometown was no different than those in mundane cities. Apparently, there was no magic that could speed up the process.

Now that I had moved back to Foxfire Haven, I had discovered the same was true of the DMV, unfortunately.

My cell phone rang as I was walking out the front door of the post office. It was Valerian Bellamy, who was both one of my roommates and a member of my coven. She was a bartender at the Sit a Spell Tavern, which was a client of mine.

"Do you have time for a last-minute pick-up?" Valerian asked me. "We just ran out of our most popular rum."

I checked my watch. It was late afternoon, but the post office run had been my last delivery for the day. My plan had been to head home and do some housecleaning, but getting in one more run would make my bank account a lot happier. The dusting could wait. "I can head to the distributor now," I said. "Do you need anything else?"

"No, just the rum. I already called ahead, so it will be waiting for you." Valerian paused. "Actually, I'm going to add whiskey to the order. Barry hasn't been in as often lately, but we're dangerously low on his go-to drink, and I'd hate to run out."

"Best not to deny a Bigfoot his favorite whiskey," I agreed. Not that I was worried about Barry getting angry if he couldn't get the expensive, single-malt whiskey he always drank at the tavern. He was a nice guy, and I usually got a quiet hello from him whenever we happened to be at the tavern at the same time.

The liquor distributor was a half-hour drive away, in the non-magical town of Stanton. By the time I had picked up the order and was on the four-lane highway back to Foxfire Haven, it was nearly dark out, and there was a gentle drizzle pelting my windshield.

From the highway, I had to take a winding, two-lane road for a few miles before it finally ran right through downtown. Sit a Spell Tavern, which was across the street from city hall, had a squat half-timber design that looked more like something from a Renaissance festival than a quaint Pacific Northwest town.

Cars were parked on both sides of the street, so I swung around to the alley that ran behind the tavern and the neighboring businesses. It was easier to get things into the kitchen and storage area from the back door, anyway. In just a few minutes, the rum and whiskey were delivered, and I was finished with work for the day.

As I was putting the empty gurney back inside the hearse, I heard a man's voice. He wasn't quite yelling, but it was close. "Are you kidding me? This is unbelievable!"

The man was pacing back and forth in front of the dumpster behind the tavern, one hand holding a phone to his ear and the other gesturing wildly as he repeated his disbelief for whatever had happened to get him so riled up. His brown hair was tousled, and as I watched, he reached up and tugged at the ends of it. The messy hair clashed with his black wool coat and plaid scarf, which both looked very expensive.

Not wanting to look like I was eavesdropping, I quickly made my way to the back door of the tavern, leaving the hearse parked where it was. I got inside and began to pull off my gloves as I headed toward the bar, but I stopped short and let my eyes rove around the dim room. Every seat at the bar that ran along one side of the tavern was occupied. The booths around the edges of the space were packed, and every table in the middle of the tavern was taken, too. I had never seen the tavern that crowded.

I attributed that to Valerian's latest potion. She called it Cold Hands, Warm Heart, and it was designed for bitter, rainy nights just like this one. It was like drinking hot chocolate, but as it traveled down your throat, a feeling of warmth spread outward, right down to the tips of your toes. It could be drunk by itself, but Valerian offered several cocktails that used the potion, including one involving a cinnamon liqueur.

At the moment, all I wanted was the potion all by itself to warm me up before I headed home. I was wondering if I could get it to go when I heard my name being called. Marlee, one of my other roommates, was waving from her seat at the bar. I hadn't noticed her before because she was nearly hidden by the gargoyles sitting on either side of her.

In fact, there were a total of five gargoyles seated at the bar, their wings neatly folded against their backs. Growing up, I'd sometimes spotted members of the gargoyle clan who lived on a big piece of wooded property outside of town. This was my first time seeing them since I'd returned to Foxfire Haven about six months before, and I'd forgotten how massive they were.

I carefully threaded my way through the crowd until I was face-to-face with Marlee, who had swiveled on her stool so her back was to the bar. "This place is packed," I said in greeting.

Marlee nodded and grinned. "Val is raking in the tips with her new potion. Everyone wants to warm up here! The gargoyles came out just to try it."

The gargoyle to Marlee's left glanced over, his sharp teeth showing in his stone-gray face as he grinned down at her. "We also came out to be social."

Marlee looked from him to me, her cheeks turning a faint shade of red. When I raised an eyebrow at her, she said quietly, "Garth here asked me if I wanted to get dinner sometime."

"And?" I prompted.

Marlee gave me a lopsided grin. "I said sure."

In response, I squeezed Marlee's arm. The four of us in our coven were about the same age. In fact, Marlee was born only six months before me, and she had just turned fifty-five. Unlike Valerian and me, Marlee had never been married. Her event business was largely built around wedding planning, and she sometimes complained that she was always the bride's planner and never the bride.

I didn't know if Garth the gargoyle was "the one" for Marlee, but he was nice-looking and had a smooth deep voice that would make dinner conversation that much better. I was excited for her.

"Other than getting a date, how are things going?" I asked Marlee as Garth turned his attention to the conversation happening on his other side.

Marlee waved a hand. "What things? I am so bored!"

I snickered. "I figured that out when you volunteered to wash and iron all the curtains at home." Most of the events Marlee planned for clients were in the warmer months, so other than some prep work for two early-spring weddings, Marlee didn't have much going on in the cold, dark days of late January. "Do we need to find someone with an immediate need for a shindig?"

"I don't mind the lack of income," Marlee explained. "I always save up for these slow months, but I can't stand the boredom. I need something to do!"

"I'm taking that plant magic class Gnorris is starting over at the garden store. I figure it's a good refresher for me after not practicing magic for almost twenty years. But it would be fun for you, too."

"I might just join you, then." Marlee brightened. "And you never know, I might meet potential clients there. When does it—"

Marlee broke off as a man stomped up to the bar, wedging himself between Marlee and Garth. I easily recognized the tousled brown hair. The man in the alley had finished his phone call and was, apparently, in need of an immediate drink.

Valerian swept up on the other side of the bar, her long white braid hanging over her right shoulder. "What would you like, Aaron? And what's wrong?"

Aaron's fingers went to his hair again. "My horrible ex-wife just showed up in town. She claims she's here for business, but I know the truth. She came here to ruin me."

CHAPTER TWO

VALERIAN GAVE AARON A skeptical look. "What makes you think your ex came here just to make you miserable?"

"I moved all the way from Florida to Washington so I could put as much distance between me and her as possible." Aaron huffed out a sigh, and I saw Marlee give her torso a little shake. I doubted anyone else noticed the faint dark-red shimmer of magic that puffed off her skin and drifted to the floor. As an empath, Marlee absorbed the emotions of others, and Aaron must have been giving off some strong emotions if Marlee was having to magically slough off what she was feeling.

"It can't be a coincidence that Wanda came to Foxfire Haven," Aaron continued.

"There are only so many magical towns," Valerian pointed out.

"What town in Florida?" I asked. After retirement, my parents had moved to the small town of Amber Beach, a sweet coastal town popular with older witches, shifters, and other supernatural creatures.

Aaron craned his neck so he could look at me. "Osbourne."

I smiled. Of course Aaron wasn't from the retirement capital of the supernatural world. "My brother lived in Osbourne for nine years, before he took a job up in Virginia. Like Val just said, there are only so many magical towns."

"Then why did she have to pick the one farthest from hers?" Aaron was tugging at his hair yet again, and I had to resist the urge to pull his hand away from his head.

"Hang on," Valerian said. "I've got a potion that will help with your agitation." She moved toward an assortment of glass bottles behind the bar, and I saw her select one with a shimmering pale-blue liquid inside. Carefully, Valerian measured a small amount of it into a pint glass, then added soda-water to it. When she handed the glass to Aaron, she said, "It's going to have a bit of a bite, so be careful on your first sip. But the garlic in it will help soothe you."

"Thanks, Val," Aaron said. "You're a gem."

"Not a well-polished one, but thanks for the compliment."

Aaron took a big swig of the drink, coughed, then opened his mouth wide so he could inhale big breaths. "So garlicky!"

"I told you it had some bite," Valerian said. As she turned toward one of the gargoyles who was trying to get her attention, I thought I saw her smiling.

Aaron gingerly sipped at his glass, then nodded. "Better." He began to move off, but he stopped and nodded at me. "Aaron Becker, by the way. We've never met."

"Hazel Underwood. I just moved back to town last summer."

Aaron looked at Marlee, then back to me. "Ah, yes. The funeral home coven, right? Grant Underwood was a good guy. He made my grandmother look great after she passed."

"My uncle was a very well-respected mortician." *Except,* I added silently, *after he began acting strange and alienated all his friends.* "Thank you."

Aaron then turned to Marlee and extended a hand. "You're the local wedding planner."

"Marlee Yamada, yes. But I also plan other events, so if you ever have a big party you need help with, you let me know."

Aaron walked off with Marlee's business card in his hand. Once he was out of earshot, she gave me a wicked look, her dark eyes lit up with excitement. "Maybe I should start telling people that wintertime parties are popular, so I can get more business in January and February."

I gestured around the full tavern. "Val's potion would have to be a part of it."

"And a bonfire," Marlee said, nodding. "Or, maybe, it should be a cozy indoor party. Flannel blankets, a roaring fire, and fun card games."

"I like this plan. I think we should head home and test flannel blankets, just to make sure you have the fluffiest, warmest ones for these winter parties."

Marlee lifted her half-drunk Cold Hands, Warm Heart potion. "We won't need any blankets after one of these."

I kept an eye on Aaron as Marlee and I chatted about our respective days. He stopped to talk to several people, who all smiled and looked glad to see him. Between the welcome reception and Valerian's potion, he seemed to be feeling better when he finally gave a wave to a table full of people, then left.

The gargoyles were on their way out, too, but not until Garth had exchanged phone numbers with Marlee. After seeing how boldly she had handed her business card to Aaron, it was surprising how shy she was about giving her number to a guy who wanted to take her on a date.

If she's ever going to find Mr. Right, we're going to have to work on her flirting skills.

The tavern seemed a lot roomier once the gargoyles were gone. They took up so much space, with their hulking bodies and broad wings. I tried to imagine how crowded the bar would have felt if Barry was there, too, brooding in his usual spot at one end.

I hopped up onto the stool Garth had just vacated. Marlee and I had both finished our potions, but neither of us was willing to head out into the cold evening just yet.

Just as I was considering making my way home, someone brushed my arm, and I looked over to see a man sliding onto the vacant stool next to me. He had a deep tan, and his blue eyes had a faded look that always made me think of weatherbeaten cowboys. The man's teeth were the most prominent part of his face. They were unnaturally white and straight, and he was showing off as many of them as he could as he grinned at Valerian.

His smile made me slightly uncomfortable, like he might try to sell me a kitchen gadget I had no need for.

Valerian seemed to feel the same. She didn't stand directly in front of him as she politely asked what he'd like to drink.

"Whiskey, please. Single malt. The best you have."

"Coming right up." She threw me a look that clearly said, *I'm glad we restocked Barry's favorite.*

When Valerian returned with the man's drink, he frowned. "Don't you have some nuts or something I can snack on?"

"No, but you can order from the menu. We've got sandwiches, fries..."

"Oh, no, I don't want anything like that. Too heavy. By the way, what year was this whiskey distilled? Some years are better than others, you know."

"I have no idea."

The man looked like he wanted to ask Valerian to check, but she gazed at him stoically until his smile faltered. I could see her fingers tapping away on the bar, a sign I'd come to recognize as annoyance. "Anything else?" Valerian asked pointedly.

"No, I'm..." The man cleared his throat. "I'm good."

"I haven't seen you here before."

The man's overly wide smile returned as he answered Valerian. "No, you haven't. I'm Ilya Dugin. I'm just in town for a week or so. I'm thinking about retirement and looking for a good place to settle down."

I heard a deep laugh behind me, followed by a man's voice. "Hazel here has just the place for you, Ilya."

"Roscoe," Valerian said in a warning tone.

"What?" Roscoe leaned forward so his head was between mine and the newcomer's. "You could live out your final years in one of Hazel's rooms, and once you're dead, you're already at the funeral home! It's a great business idea."

"It's not a working funeral home anymore," I reminded Roscoe. Of course, he knew that already. He'd been close friends with Uncle Grant for years, right up until Grant's behavior grew too strange for him. I wanted to swat the old man out of my personal space, but I was too polite for that. Instead, I did my best to ignore his smug laugh.

"On second thought," Roscoe said, his voice taking on an especially malicious tone, "it's probably better that you don't rub elbows with Hazel. You might end up dead."

"And what's that supposed to mean?" Marlee asked, looking indignant on my behalf.

Roscoe shrugged languidly. "It means there weren't so many murders in Foxfire Haven before she came back here."

I opened my mouth to protest, then reminded myself I was supposed to be ignoring Roscoe. He moved off a few seconds later, when it became clear I wasn't going to take the bait.

"Roscoe is an old meanie," I told Ilya. "If you do decide to retire here, I recommend not hanging out with him."

He laughed. "You don't have to worry about that. I prefer people a little closer to my age."

If I'd had to guess, I would have said Ilya was somewhere in his early forties, so he was probably about a decade younger than me. That meant Roscoe was old enough to be his dad.

Roscoe was old enough to be mine, for that matter.

I felt a wave of gratitude that I'd had such a caring dad, and not a jerk like Roscoe. Even though it had been years since Dad died, he was always in my heart.

"Oh, Hazel." Marlee put an arm around my shoulders. "Roscoe made you sad!"

I laughed at that. "No, that is definitely not the feeling I get whenever he's around. I was just missing my dad, who was the total opposite of Roscoe." I slid off the stool. "I'm going to head home. Perkins probably wonders what's happened to me."

"Tell Stella that I'll be home soon, too." Marlee winked at me, though I knew she wasn't joking. Her toucan would understand every word I said. "One of my clients is in the booth by the door, so I want to stop and chat with her before I head out."

"See you there." I nodded at the man searching for a town to retire to, wondering why anyone younger than me would already be looking into that.

Maybe he's got enough money to retire early. Lucky guy.

I was still thinking about everything from my dad to early retirement when I pulled into the circular driveway in front of the funeral home. Uncle Grant had been the last in a long line of funeral directors who both lived and worked in the sprawling brick building. After Grant's death, the town's new funeral director had opened a much more modern facility on the opposite side of town. It didn't have as much character as the place I'd inherited, but since it wasn't a century old, it probably didn't have the constant repair bills, either.

The headlights of my vintage hearse swept across the front porch. Between two of the tall white columns, I spotted a person standing at the front door. It was only then I noticed a small, black sedan parked to one side.

Usually, I would drive along the narrow path that led to the detached garage in the backyard, but since I had unexpected company, I pulled right up in front of the porch steps.

As soon as I climbed out of the hearse, I could see it was a woman standing on the porch. Her mouth hung open as she stared at my unusual form of transportation.

"Hi. Can I help you?" I called.

The woman slowly closed her mouth, then turned her eyes to me. "Yes. Hi. What kind of money are we talking about?"

"You mean my delivery rates?" I asked. Most customers simply called to ask that question, instead of showing up on my doorstep at five o'clock in the evening. Maybe, I thought, this woman had an immediate and urgent need for a delivery. "It depends on how far I need to drive, and—"

"No," the woman interrupted, looking as confused as I felt. "I mean for this place."

After I had realized I would need extra income to maintain the old funeral home, I posted flyers around town for roommates. I had quickly filled the three available rooms, and I thought I had taken down all the flyers. I figured I must have missed one somewhere.

"I'm sorry, but all the rooms are rented already."

"Rooms?" The woman laughed, her bleach-blond waves bouncing against her shoulders. "No, I meant, how much money to buy this whole place?"

CHAPTER THREE

IT WAS MY TURN to stare, open-mouthed, as I processed what the woman had just said to me. Finally, with an effort, I told her, "My home is not for sale."

The woman laughed again. The porch light was enough for me to see the mirth in her green eyes. "My boss says everything is for sale! It's just a matter of negotiation."

"I guess your boss has never met anyone with a sentimental attachment to a funeral home, then."

The woman's smile disappeared, and she glanced over her shoulder at the front door, like a dead body might open it for her at any moment.

"What makes you interested in this place?" I continued. It was not, I knew from her expression, the home's history.

"I'm not. My boss and I were driving around town today, exploring different neighborhoods, and she decided this is the house she wants to buy. She likes plenty of space."

"You and your boss are new to Foxfire Haven, then." On a hunch, I added, "You're from Florida, right?"

The woman's eyes widened. "Yes! How did you know?"

"Just a guess." After Aaron complained that his ex had just shown up in town, and that she was from Florida, I had to wonder if he'd been married to this woman or to her boss. My money was on the boss, since the woman on my porch seemed a bit too young for Aaron. She looked like she might be in her mid-thirties.

The woman didn't seem to find my correct guess about her home state odd in the slightest. Of course, being in the magical world, she might have simply thought I was psychic. "It looks like we might be relocating here, yes," she said.

"We?"

"Me and my boss."

I tilted my head. "You move wherever your boss does?"

"I'm her personal assistant. I have to go where she goes. By the way, I'm Nicole. Nicole Murrow."

"Hazel Underwood." I almost asked Nicole if she knew Aaron, then reminded myself it was none of my business. So, instead, I got back to the matter at hand. "I'm flattered your boss liked the look of the funeral home, but like I said, it's not for sale."

"Honestly, its history might have been a dealbreaker, anyway." Nicole threw another uneasy glance at the front door, then eyed the hearse. "That came with the funeral home?"

"Yeah. It was my uncle's. He was the funeral director here for decades."

"Decades." Nicole gave an exaggerated shiver. "I don't think she would want to live in a place where so many dead people have been."

"Well, good luck in your continued search. Er, her search. I hope she finds a place that's both big and free of embalming rooms."

"Thanks." Nicole pulled her thin coat tighter around her body. "It's cold here."

"Welcome to Washington in January. One of my roommates is a bartender at the Sit a Spell Tavern. She's got a Cold Hands, Warm Heart potion that's guaranteed to shake off the chill."

Nicole's face brightened. "That sounds perfect. And I can ask some of the patrons if they know of any big houses for sale around here. Thanks!"

Nicole practically bounced down the steps, looking eager to get to the tavern. I watched as she got into her car and slowly drove away, wondering if I should have quoted her an astronomical price. Would I sell the funeral home if I could get millions for it?

I left the hearse where it was, too tired for the moment to drive it to the garage. Instead, I went inside the house and threw myself down onto the sofa in the living room.

I didn't realize I had fallen asleep until I heard Marlee calling my name softly. I cracked one eye open. "I am too old to nap on the couch," I mumbled. My left hip was protesting loudly.

"Class starts in thirty minutes," Marlee said.

I sat up, my grogginess disappearing. I had slept for more than an hour. I heard a quiet trill and looked over to see Perkins, my familiar, perched on one arm of the sofa. He ruffled up his brown and cream feathers, although, as a burrowing owl, he looked tiny no matter how hard he tried.

"He was tapping on your head with his beak, but you were out cold," Marlee told me. "He had to come get me to wake you up."

"Thanks, Perky. And thanks, Marlee. Let me scarf down a snack, then we can get going."

In just fifteen minutes, Marlee and I were on our way to the Growing Power Garden Store. I was driving, figuring I could put the hearse in the garage when we got home from the plant magic class.

I had been eager to leave Foxfire Haven after high school graduation. I wanted to go to college in a big city, where there were lots of people and a never-ending stream of things to do. Living in San Francisco had been great, with one exception: I was an oddity in the mundane world. After my daughter and some friends had seen me doing magic one night, Tara's social life at school had been precarious for a bit. Since she was so embarrassed by having a witch for a mother, I had given up my magic.

As much as I could, at any rate. There was no stopping magic, and since I wasn't using it for spell work anymore, my magic would build up inside me. Usually, I could control how it was expended.

But it only took one accident to ruin everything. We'd been at my granddaughter's dance recital when one of the teachers had tripped and fallen off the stage. My adrenaline had shot up, along with my magic, and that magic had exploded out of my body with so much force that several people were knocked off their feet.

It was impossible to explain to an auditorium full of non-magical people that I had just experienced uncontrolled magical shedding. Most of the parents and children thought witches were just characters in fairy tales. And they would have thought I was joking if I said I was friends with a Bigfoot.

So, I had slunk back to Foxfire Haven, where I might get teased if my magic got out of my control, but I wouldn't create a scandal. I was learning to use my magic again, and things like this magical plant class were a good way for me to remember everything I had learned growing up.

Marlee had a smile on her face the entire drive to the plant store. When I asked her what was making her so happy, she replied, "My boredom ends right now! I'm really glad you suggested I join you for this class. Jo is going to cover it for the newspaper, so she'll be there, too."

"Too bad Val can't join us." I resisted the urge to ask Marlee if her happiness also had something to do with the prospect of a date.

When we walked inside the garden store, though, we were both surprised to see Valerian was there, talking to a few other attendees. Apparently, our entire coven would be taking the class.

"I thought you were working a double shift tonight," I said.

"I am working!" Valerian hooked her thumbs in the straps of her faded red overalls. "I'm your guest instructor tonight. The tavern was kind enough to loan me out."

Gnorris, the owner of the store, was standing on top of an upturned planter nearby, which made him appear only a head shorter than Marlee, who was the most petite member of our coven.

Gnorris nodded toward Valerian, his red conical hat seeming to point at her. "Val is going to give us some tips about making plant-based potions."

"Aren't all potions plant-based?" I asked.

Gnorris gave his long white beard a tug. "I'm partial to a concoction that uses chicken stock."

"I'm pretty sure that's a soup, not a potion," I commented.

"Only if you drink it hot." Gnorris planted his hands on his hips and gave me a look that was half-teasing, half-exasperation. Since gnomes were only about as tall as my knees, though, it was hard to feel intimidated by him.

"Oh, do we get to work with mugwort tonight?" Marlee asked. She was looking at a table packed with small pots of plants that had long stems covered in green leaves.

Gnorris pivoted on the upturned planter so he could see where Marlee was looking. "Yes, it's great for new beginnings, among other things, so I thought it would be a good start for this class." He glanced at his watch. "Speaking of starting, it's time."

There were about fifteen of us there, and Gnorris raised his voice to be heard over the din of all the conversations. Soon, he had all of us lined up on stools at high-top wooden tables, which usually held pots of flowers for sale. The flowers had all been removed, though, giving us plenty of workspace.

After a quick introduction, Gnorris asked two people to pass out the pots of mugwort. As soon as we had those in front of us, he began, "Valerian Bellamy was kind enough to come tonight to tell us about potion-making, and mugwort is commonly used in potions. When you need a fresh start, psychic protection, or enhanced divination skills, mugwort is a great ingredient to include. But, before you can make a potion or do any spell work with it, you need to know how to cultivate it. The soil should be loose, not packed in tight."

As Gnorris continued, Jo slid into the room, walking carefully to make as little sound as possible. She joined Marlee and me at our table, gave us a wave, then pulled out the small notebook and pen she always had with her. She quickly started making notes for her newspaper story as Gnorris spoke.

Once Gnorris had given us the rundown of how to care for mugwort, it was time to repot them. An array of colorful clay pots was sitting to one side, and Gnorris told us to pick a color that corresponded to the kind of magic we wanted to do.

I was wrist-deep in soil, transferring my mugwort to a gray planter to encourage mugwort's psychic protection aspects, when Valerian came over to see how it was going with her coven.

"Now that we're all here," I said, "I can tell you my news. Someone came to the house to inquire about buying the funeral home."

Marlee and Valerian gasped, but Jo's eyebrows drew down. "Let me guess: your visitor was a tall woman with a voice like a foghorn."

"No. She was a regular-sized blonde who sounded more like a news anchor. You know, well-spoken but maybe a little too high on the perky scale."

Before I could add that Nicole had been scouting out the house for someone else, Marlee said, "Who are you thinking of, Jo?"

Jo put her clay pot down so hard I worried it might have cracked. She swept her long black braids over her shoulder, the purple streaks in them shining in the bright fluorescent lights overhead. "The woman who's trying to get between me and my career."

Chapter Four

Valerian crossed her arms, her blue eyes blazing. "Who is this foghorn, and why is she trying to interfere with your job?"

"Wanda Whitcomb." Jo grabbed her mugwort and yanked it out of the dirt. "She showed up at the newspaper office and started telling Sam that she wanted the whole operation, and he was going to sell it to her."

"I find that unlikely," Marlee said. "I've been advertising with the *Foxfire Haven Recorder* for years now, and Sam Doane isn't going to let just anyone buy it from him."

"He's both the editor and publisher, right?" I asked. "He wasn't in charge back when I was growing up here."

Jo shook her head. "No, the paper was founded around the same time the town was. It's had about eight owners over the decades. But all of them have been members of the Foxfire Haven community. People who knew their neighbors and didn't just want to...want to... Honestly, I don't know what Wanda wants to do with the paper. Sam says she hinted that she thought we could be bringing in a lot more advertising revenue, so maybe she thinks she can make a boatload of money with it."

"Nicole, the woman who wanted to know what the price for the funeral home was, said she's a personal assistant for a woman who might be relocating here," I said. "I'm guessing that woman is Wanda. We were just talking to Wanda's ex-husband at the tavern this afternoon, and he's furious she's in town."

"Oh, Aaron's ex, huh?" Valerian shook her head. "She sounds like a steamroller."

"And she apparently has some line about how everything is for sale, and it's just a matter of negotiation." I rolled my eyes at the memory of my ridiculous conversation with Nicole.

"Wanda said the exact same thing to Sam!" Jo had scattered soil across her notebook, and when she picked it up, it sent the soil flying. "Sorry, sorry. I'm just worked up about this whole thing."

"Clearly," Marlee said as she brushed bits of dirt from her sweater. "What did Sam say to Wanda's offer?"

Instead of an answer, we all heard a loud clap. Gnorris was calling the class back to attention. "Now that we've learned the basics, Valerian is going to give us some pointers for how to use mugwort in potions."

Valerian squeezed Jo's arm. "It's going to turn out just fine," she whispered. Then, she turned and walked to the front of the room, looking right at home in her dirt-streaked overalls.

"Let's start with how to harvest the leaves for potions," Valerian said in a voice loud enough to be heard by the entire class. "Don't just yank the leaves off the stalks, or you're going to have bruising. That will reduce the magical effect, and it will make it harder for new leaves to grow back in those spots. Instead, you want to use sharp scissors or, if you really want to amp up the magic, a small silver knife that's been attuned to your desired outcome."

It had been so long since I'd heard that terminology that I had to think back to what "attuned" even meant. By the time I remembered it meant the knife's blade should be coated in an oil blend specific to the spell to be performed with it, I had missed what Valerian said about how to properly store the leaves.

Learning magic as a kid had felt so easy and fun. Now, as a middle-aged witch trying to relearn it all, there were a lot of moments that were downright difficult. All the things that had come so naturally to me once upon a time now took effort.

Marlee must have sensed my frustration, because she leaned toward me and said, "You've already made so much progress since you came back to town. Be patient, and this will get to be easy again, too."

I let go of my mugwort so I could wrap my arms around Marlee in a hug. I was careful, of course, not to get my dirty hands on her sweater. Having an empath for a roommate was a real bonus, because she could feel exactly what I was feeling and know the right words to comfort me.

After that, I focused on Valerian's instructions. Even if I didn't retain every bit of the knowledge she was sharing, this was valuable for me, and I was still making progress with rekindling my magic.

Valerian wrapped up with a detailed description of how to get the most magic and flavor out of the leaves, so a potion would be both effective and tasty. Then, she and Gnorris walked around the room, giving pointers as we all tried our hand at the process.

"Back to the offer on the newspaper," Marlee said as she carefully cut some leaves off her plant. "What did Sam tell Wanda?"

Jo laid seven leaves onto the table and began to press them with her thumbs, as Valerian had instructed. "Luckily, Sam held firm that he doesn't want to sell. But something tells me Wanda isn't the type to take no for an answer. If anything, I think Sam's refusal just made her that much more determined to win. Apparently, she even referred to herself as a publishing witch and claimed only her magic could save the paper. As if we need saving!"

"Careful, Jo!" We all looked down to see Gnorris standing near Jo, both hands reaching up toward the tabletop. "You're going to mangle your leaves if you press them that hard!"

Jo glanced at the leaves, which she had torn in her agitation. "Oops."

"It's okay," Gnorris said. "Just snip a few fresh leaves off your plant and try again." He moved off, and I heard him say "Excellent work!" to a man standing at the table next to us.

Gnorris hadn't complimented me, but he also hadn't made any corrections, so I took that as a sign that I was doing all right for myself.

Valerian was also making her way around the room, and she arrived at our table while I was eavesdropping on Gnorris's praise for the group next to us.

"Okay, Jo, spill it," Valerian commanded. "Even if Sam winds up selling the newspaper, how is this Wanda going to ruin your career? You made it sound awfully dire."

Jo stopped trimming leaves from her plant, and she put the scissors down. I figured she was doing that so she wouldn't accidentally crush the next batch into oblivion, too. "It's just... Well, Sam and I haven't actually discussed it, but I want to take over the newspaper when he retires."

Valerian gave Jo a sympathetic look, but in her usual practical tone, she said, "Even if the worst-case scenario happens, and Sam sells out to Wanda, you still have a great career as a journalist. And who knows? Maybe Wanda will be content to act as publisher, and she'll hire you as the editor."

Jo shook her head. "I don't think I'd want to work for her, even if she did offer me that position." She laid both hands flat on the table. "There is no way I can keep discussing this without wrecking the potion I'm making. I'm going to step outside and do a quick focus spell."

We all offered to join Jo, but she insisted that we should stay and continue working on our own mugwort potions. When she rejoined us five minutes later, she looked much calmer, and she managed to get her leaves prepared properly. Gnorris even praised her work the next time he came by our table.

Class ended with all of us toasting to our success and drinking our potions. Since mine was designed to induce psychic protection, it was a nice way to end our first night of learning plant magic. I felt safe, even from strangers who showed up on my doorstep, like Nicole.

Marlee, Jo, and I all tried each other's potions. Mine was slightly bitter compared to theirs, but overall, I felt like I'd done a decent job. Since Valerian was our potions expert, I asked her what I'd done wrong. She took a sip, then smiled and said, "I think it's your plant, and not you. If I was going to sell this to a customer at the tavern, I'd add a touch of maple syrup."

Once class had wrapped up, we all headed for our cars. Jo and Valerian got home and settled inside the funeral home before Marlee and me, though, since I was still agonizingly slow at parking the hearse in the garage. I had gotten much better at navigating around town in that hulking vehicle, but I was still getting the hang of sliding it into tight spaces.

Marlee and I walked through the back door into the kitchen to find Holman staring down Valerian and Jo. Holman had his back to us, but since he was a ghost and slightly transparent, I could see the pursed lips and drawn-down eyebrows on both Jo's and Valerian's faces.

"Holman, who are you criticizing, and why?" I asked as I unbuttoned my coat.

Holman turned toward me, every one of his wavy blond hairs perfectly in place. Even his pencil mustache looked like it had been trimmed using a ruler. "I was just saying that the two of them are a mess. It looks like they've been foraging in the woods."

"We were at a plant magic class," I explained.

Holman waved toward me, and I looked down to see bits of mugwort leaves stuck to my sweatshirt. "So I see."

"Oh, please," Marlee said. She had lived with us for a while before finally meeting Holman, who had been the funeral director there in the nineteen twenties and thirties. Her excitement about living with a ghost had quickly been dampened by his attitude. She gestured toward Holman's immaculate light-gray suit, which had the wide padded shoulders and nipped-waist style that had been popular in the nineteen thirties. "Like you never got messy while working."

"I wore an apron, of course," Holman sneered. He ran a hand down his jacket. "My suits were far too expensive to risk them coming into contact with my clients."

"You mean with the dead bodies," Valerian intoned.

"They were still my clients."

"Good night, Holman," I said pointedly. "Come back when you have something nice to say."

"Put more care into your appearance, and I will." With that, Holman disappeared.

"I don't even care," Jo said. "Holman knows how to get under my skin, but I am simply too exhausted to be offended tonight."

We all agreed, and a few minutes later, I was in my room, pulling my pajamas out of my drawer.

It was only after I had changed that I realized I had forgotten to feed Perkins. I really was exhausted. Delivery runs, bizarre encounters at both the tavern and on my own front porch, plus a class about magic had completely drained me.

When I went back into the kitchen, I found Perkins curled up in his nest, which I had made for him out of scraps of flannel material. He tilted his head at me, giving me a reproachful look. However, he wasn't the only one in the kitchen. Jo was there, sitting at the little table in the breakfast nook.

As I prepared a small dish of food for Perkins, I said softly, "I thought you were heading to bed, too."

"I will, once my brain stops running at a hundred miles an hour."

I put the dish of food down on the windowsill, and Perkins hopped over to begin eating. I gave him a scratch on the head, then sat down opposite Jo. "Maybe talking about whatever's on your brain will help it slow down."

Jo sighed. Behind her, there was a flash of white as her familiar, Gordon, swooped through the window we always kept half open. The pelican seemed to know Jo needed comfort. He landed on the table, sending a pile of receipts Jo had left there flying, then tilted his head downward until the tip of his beak touched Jo's arm.

"I love being a writer," Jo said after a moment.

"But?"

"If I don't become editor of the *Foxfire Haven Recorder* someday, I'll look like a fool."

I leaned forward and reached a hand across the table, putting my fingers on top of Jo's. "It will be bad luck if Wanda gets in the way of your career goals, but why do you think it will make you look like a fool?"

Jo breathed in deeply, then formed her lips into an *O* and let it out slowly. "Because I turned down a position as associate editor of the *Vesta Falls Journal*, with a clear path to becoming senior editor in a handful of years. It's a bigger paper in a bigger city. Everyone told me I was stupid to stay in Foxfire Haven."

Chapter Five

I WANTED TO ASK Jo for a list of every single person who had judged her so harshly for her decision, so I could go knock on their doors and give them a lecture. With a huff, I leaned back and crossed my arms over my chest. “Who is everyone?”

“Family, mostly. Plus, well, I was dating a guy at the time, and he wasn’t happy about me turning down such a huge opportunity.”

“Why did you turn down the job offer?” Vesta Falls was one of the biggest magical towns on the West Coast, and living and working there really would have been a huge opportunity for Jo.

“I love this town.” Jo sat back in her chair and gazed up at the ceiling. “I came here when I was a cub reporter, fresh out of college, and I fell in love with Foxfire Haven. The people, all the gorgeous nature around here, how cute our downtown is, all of it. My dream isn’t just to be an editor of a newspaper. I want to be editor of *this* newspaper. Sam is already talking about retiring in the next few years, but what if he takes the buyout instead?”

"You said you and Sam have never discussed your dream of filling his role someday," I said gently. "You need to tell him."

"Yeah. I do. I will." Jo nodded once, then opened her arms so Gordon could pad closer to her on his giant webbed feet. She gathered him up in a hug and pressed her face against his back. He looked like a fluffy white pillow but with a giant beak. "I just feel so helpless."

"You're never helpless. You have your coven, and a ton of friends in this town. Plus, you have magic."

Jo lifted her head and gave me a bright look. "Of course! I can manifest Wanda right out of town!"

I raised my hands. "Whoa! I don't know about that!"

Jo's magical talent was in manifesting. What she wrote down with intention became reality. Unfortunately for her, those intentions had a habit of backfiring in unexpected ways. They would succeed but often not in the way Jo had anticipated.

"I'll be very careful in my choice of words," Jo promised.

"I was thinking we could do a group spell for a positive outcome in this situation."

Jo was nodding, and she reached past Gordon to fish her notebook and pen out of her purse, which was lying on the table. She flipped the notebook open to a blank page and began to scribble hastily. "We should do that. Absolutely. I'm also going to think about what I could write that couldn't possibly go awry."

I knew the look in Jo's eyes. There would be no arguing with her on this, so I stood up and said, "Just don't lose too much sleep thinking about it. You need a clear mind before you write any intention."

Jo stopped writing long enough to spare me a glance. "I'm just jotting down a few thoughts, and then I'll go to bed. Promise."

Jo was absent at the breakfast table the next morning, and I figured she had stayed up later than she should have, pondering what kind of intention she could write down that couldn't possibly go wrong. Marlee and Valerian were there, though, both already halfway through a cup of coffee by the time I joined them.

I was tempted to tell them about my conversation with Jo the night before, but I knew it was her story to tell, not mine. If she wanted the rest of the coven to know about her career goals and the doubts her loved ones had expressed about turning down the job at the *Vesta Falls Journal*, then she could tell them when she was ready.

No sooner had I taken my first sip of coffee than the doorbell rang. I took my cup with me as I trudged toward the front door. It wasn't even eight o'clock yet, so who could possibly be at the door? I didn't have anyone coming to do repair work on the house that day.

At least, I didn't think so.

I reached the long, wide hallway that led from the back of the house—where funeral directors had lived—to the front, where the business part of putting on funerals had taken place. The two chapels, former casket showroom, and Uncle Grant's office were all off the main hallway, which was decorated with faded—but still pretty—floral wallpaper and a plush burgundy carpet.

And, as soon as I turned into the hallway, I stopped short. The front door was standing wide open.

Again.

The door had been opening of its own accord for months, and our best guess was that there was another ghost haunting the house, even though it wasn't making its presence known in any other way. Holman said he hadn't detected another paranormal presence, though, so we were still trying to figure out the mystery of the opening door.

The doorbell, however, had not rung of its own accord. Standing in the open doorway was Chief Constable Wyatt Hightower. He was wearing his crisp gray uniform shirt and black trousers, plus a black jacket emblazoned with an embroidered logo for the Foxfire Haven Constables. His badge, a silver pentagram surrounded by a circle, was hidden by the jacket, but I knew it was there, pinned to the left breast of his shirt.

"Hello, Hazel," Wyatt called down the hallway.

I was still standing at the opposite end, and with a sense of resignation, I made my way toward Wyatt. "Good morning. Come on in."

Wyatt gave a little shake of his head. "No need. I noticed your front door was open again as I was on my way to the station. I figured I should let you know. Your house will be freezing if you don't close it."

This could have been a text, I thought grumpily. Seeing Wyatt always made me feel extra snarky. Our relationship hadn't gotten off on the best foot, since his cat had been after Perkins, and although we mostly got along now, there was still tension between us. We seemed to know exactly how to push each other's buttons.

I was making an effort to be nicer to Wyatt, though, so I lifted my cup. "You want some coffee? I've even got travel mugs in the kitchen, if you want to take it to work."

Wyatt gazed at me with his ice-blue eyes, and it felt like he was looking into me rather than at me. I couldn't imagine why an offer of coffee deserved such a scrutinizing stare. "No," he finally said. "But thanks." He ran a hand through his silver hair. "I, uh... You and your roommates doing all right?"

"Okay, I suppose. Jo has some drama at the newspaper, but otherwise, we're all good."

"Yeah, I heard about that. Sam's not going anywhere, if you ask me. He's a stubborn old man."

"Takes one to know one," I said. With a gasp, I slapped my free hand over my mouth. I moved it just enough to say, "Sorry. It just came out."

The skin around Wyatt's eyes crinkled as he laughed. "You're not wrong. This stubborn old man needs to get to work. Have a nice day."

Wyatt had already turned around by the time I was able to wish him the same. I could feel my cheeks burning as I watched him descend the porch steps and climb into his old sedan.

It was the first time I had seen Wyatt in a few weeks, and the encounter left me feeling strangely odd. It had been almost nice to see him. Even though he was the grumpiest man in all of Foxfire Haven, there were times when he wasn't so bad.

I shut the door, locked it, then returned to the kitchen, wondering how long it would be before the door was wide open again.

Jo had joined the others by then, and she was partway through telling them her story about turning down the associate editor position with the *Vesta Falls Journal* and her family's disapproval of the decision. She cut off when I sat back down and asked, "What did the chief constable want? I spotted you two as I was walking to the kitchen."

"Nothing. He was letting me know the front door was open again."

"He stopped to tell you that?" Valerian tapped a fingernail against her cell phone, which was lying on the table next to her plate of half-eaten toast. "Seems like he could have just called or texted."

"I thought the same thing!" I said.

"He missed you," Marlee teased in a singsong tone. "Your boyfriend missed you, Hazel."

"He's not even my friend, let alone my boyfriend," I countered.

Valerian laughed. "You and Wyatt are friends, whether you like it or not."

"Hmm. Anyway, I guess we all need to check on the front door from time to time. As Wyatt wisely pointed out, our home will be as cold as it is outside if we're not vigilant."

"We're on it," Marlee promised. "Jo said you thought a spell for a positive outcome to this newspaper business might be in order. I agree, and I have just the spell for it."

"You have a Get Wanda Gone spell?" Valerian asked.

"Val! No, I have my Happily Ever After spell." Marlee was shaking her head disapprovingly at Valerian, her sleek black ponytail wagging with the motion, but she was also smiling. "I've helped wedding clients perform it at their receptions. With a few small modifications, we can make it fit Jo's situation."

"Fine, then," Valerian said. "But, if Jo wants it, I also have a potion that can stop Wanda in her tracks!"

"I'm tempted," Jo admitted, "but we want a happily ever after for everyone. Do no harm, remember?"

Valerian sighed dramatically. "I know, I know. The first rule of witchcraft."

As we moved on to talking about the day ahead, I felt a warmth that was far different than the one that had bloomed in my cheeks just a few minutes before, when I had accidentally insulted Wyatt. My roommates, my coven, my friends. It felt good to have them around me, and to start my day with some laughter. We all knew Valerian was just kidding. She could be almost as grumpy as Wyatt sometimes, but she wouldn't really hurt anyone.

My first delivery of the day was scheduled for ten o'clock. Stacy's Stationery and Sundries had become a regular customer, and it was fairly easy work. I simply loaded up on stock at Stacy's storage unit, then shuttled it to her store.

That day's delivery was on track to be the usual routine job. At the storage unit, I had loaded three boxes of self-warming teacups onto the gurney, a shopping bag full of crochet book bags, plus a plastic bin full of elegant fountain pens. I got them over to Stacy's and helped her load them into the small storage room in the back of her shop.

On my way out, I paused to peruse a wall display of greeting cards. My brother's birthday would be coming up in just a few weeks, so I wanted to find a card that would match his wry sense of humor.

I was looking at a card featuring an illustration of a cat waving a wand when I heard a raised voice by the cash register. "Oh, I'm sure you can accommodate me," a deep, resonant woman's voice said.

I knew without turning around that it was Wanda. Jo had been right: the woman really did sound like a foghorn.

Stacy said something that was too quiet for me to hear, and then Wanda continued, "In a shop like this? Nonsense! Just look at the items on these shelves!"

Wanda was turning to wave a hand toward a display of fine stationery right as I was turning toward the cash register. Our eyes met, my gray ones and Wanda's piercing brown ones.

"That's your hearse outside," Wanda said to me.

When I nodded, she added, "You're the delivery lady who lives at the funeral home. How much?"

So much for the idea she'd be put off by the dead bodies.

"It's not for sale. Sorry."

Wanda clearly didn't like that answer. She stalked over to me, and I retreated until my back was up against the wall of greeting cards. Her halo of thick, short brown curls shook with her determination as she leaned in toward me. "Everything has a price. It's just a matter of negotiation. You could buy yourself a nice house anywhere with what I'd be willing to pay."

"My home is not for sale," I reiterated.

"Nonsense!"

It was, I decided, Wanda's favorite word.

I could feel Wanda's breath on my face as she moved even closer to me. "Give me a number, and we'll start negotiating. That's how this works."

Maybe, I thought, *I don't want her to get a happily ever after.*

CHAPTER SIX

I IMMEDIATELY FELT GUILTY for thinking that, and I remembered our conversation at the breakfast table just that morning. *Do no harm* was the first rule of witchcraft. The second was, unofficially, *don't do love spells*, but I definitely wasn't tempted to work one of those on Wanda.

I'm a witch, not a villain, I told myself firmly. Besides, I needed to be polite since I was in front of a customer. So, in the most sedate voice I could muster, I said, "Please, excuse me. I'm working right now. The funeral home is part of my family legacy, and it is not for sale. Have a good day."

I wiggled sideways so I could get out of the line of Wanda's intense gaze. It was no wonder Jo had zero interest in working for her. She was a bully, plain and simple. In fact, I realized, she would probably get along great with the mayor of Foxfire Haven. Euphoria Lachlan had been my high school bully, and she and Wanda likely had a lot in common.

Wanda began shouting numbers at me, but I walked away from her, not looking over my shoulder once. "You okay?" I asked Stacy as I reached the cash register.

Stacy looked shaken, but she nodded and gave me a small smile. "I'm fine. You head on out, and I'll see you next week."

Instead of going home, I decided to stop by the tavern. Valerian was working the midday shift, and I knew she'd give me a sympathetic ear.

Except, before going anywhere, my first order of business was shedding all the magic that had built up during that confrontation with Wanda. The more threatened by her I'd felt, the more my magic had built up, ready to be deployed if necessary. If I didn't get rid of the excess, it would find its way out in some public, embarrassing way.

I didn't want Wanda to spot me—or anyone, for that matter—so I drove the hearse to the tavern, parked on the curb out front, then ducked down a narrow lane that led to the alley out behind the tavern and the other buildings along that side of Main Street. The small space between a parked van and a recycling bin would give me adequate privacy.

After focusing my thoughts on what I needed to do, I quietly recited the words to shed my magic. Soon, a puff of pink magic radiated off my body, and it shimmered in the watery sunlight that filtered through the high gray clouds overhead.

That feels better.

I waited a few minutes while my magic drifted to the dirty ground below and slowly dissipated. Meanwhile, I took deep breaths and enjoyed the feeling of relief.

When I walked inside the tavern, I made a beeline for the bar and easily found a spot on a stool. It was a bit too early for lunch, so there were only a few people scattered around the tavern.

Barry was there, sitting on the same stool he always occupied at the end of the bar. He, however, wasn't eating lunch. He was hunched over his usual glass of expensive single-malt whiskey. He turned to me as I was settling in. "Good to see you, Hazel."

"You, too, Barry. Everything good?"

Barry gazed at me thoughtfully with his golden-brown eyes, which were just a shade darker than his honey-colored fur. Finally, he nodded. "Things are better."

I knew Barry was getting over a recent breakup, and it sounded like he was beginning to recover from the grief of it. He wasn't coming into the tavern as often, and the fact that he was saying anything at all was a sign of how much better he was feeling.

Valerian swept up to me with a pint glass that had a pale-blue vapor curling up out of it. "Here," she said, plunking it down in front of me. "You need this."

"How do you know, and what is it?"

Valerian tilted her head at me. "I may not be an empath, like Marlee, but I am a part of your coven. I can tell when your emotions are on a tightrope. This is similar to the potion I served Aaron yesterday. It will help calm you."

"I met Wanda."

"Oh." Valerian drew it out, expressing a lot with that one word.

Since Valerian wasn't busy taking care of patrons, I dove into the tale of my encounter with Wanda. When I was finished, Valerian drummed her fingers on the bar. "I know we had that whole do no harm chat..."

"Believe me, I had the same conversation with myself."

"If she comes in here, I'm slipping a Mind Your Own Business potion into her drink!"

"Do you really have something like that?" As soon as I had asked that, though, I added, "No, never mind. We aren't doing anything mean to Wanda. We'll do that spell for Jo tonight, like we planned."

"Happily ever after," Valerian muttered.

"I don't mean to eavesdrop," Barry said, leaning toward us, "but is this about the woman who's looking to buy the newspaper?"

"You've heard the gossip, huh?" I winked at Barry, because he had once told me how little he liked being the subject of local tongue-wagging.

"I met her. Ran into her at the bookstore." Barry shuddered. "I'm more than seven feet tall, and even I was intimidated by her."

I couldn't imagine Barry being scared of anyone, or anything. Wanda must have made quite an impression.

"So, Val," Barry continued, "if you do decide to add that Mind Your Own Business potion to her drink, I'll gladly pay for it."

Barry turned back to his whiskey, leaving Valerian and me chuckling.

Marlee joined us not long after, stomping her way across the floor. When she reached us, she said, "It's a no-go for the spell tonight. The magic store is completely out of borage, and they don't know when they'll get more in. I did get a new aquamarine crystal to use for the spell, though. It was too pretty to pass up."

"How long until Adeline gets more in stock?" I asked.

"The guy working there today says there's a shipment coming in a week."

"That might be too late to help Jo," Valerian said. "I guess we need to find a Plan B."

"I have plenty of borage," Barry said. "I keep it in pots, so I can bring it inside during the winter, and it's been thriving. I'd be happy to give you however much you need for your spell. Just drop by anytime this afternoon."

"Thanks, Barry!" I enthused. "I'll do that. Maybe around three?"

"Sure." With that, Barry slid his empty glass toward Valerian's side of the bar and stood. "See you then."

Marlee was staring at Barry as he lumbered out of the tavern. She was used to him being the silent, brooding type. "What just happened?" she asked slowly.

"Barry has been warming up lately," Valerian said.

"Wow. Did your Cold Hands, Warm Heart potion do that, Val?" Marlee was still staring toward the door, even though Barry was already gone.

"No." Valerian made a surprised noise. "Maybe. Oh, wouldn't that be nice if it had a side-effect that made people's personalities more warm and outgoing?"

"Don't give it to Wanda, then!" I said. "She's outgoing enough as it is."

As Marlee and I ate sandwiches, I filled her in on my morning. She agreed with me that the sooner we did the spell, the better.

After lunch, I had a delivery that was a little more complicated than my run for Stacy. I had to go to a cafe on the outskirts of town to pick up their Christmas decorations, shuttle them to the owner's house, then head to a restaurant supply store the next town over to pick up an order of to-go containers and other items.

By the time I had returned to the cafe with their order, it was nearly three o'clock already, so I drove straight to Barry's house afterward. He lived in a sweet cabin he'd built himself in a clearing of the forest, and the wild garden that grew right up to the walls made the whole place feel like something out of a fantasy movie. The first and only time I'd been there had been when Barry hired me to haul away some things, and I could feel the magic of the place then. It wasn't witchcraft but something even more elemental and ancient.

When I knocked on the door of the cabin, I expected Barry to open it and hand me a bundle of borage. He was a very private person, so it surprised me when he waved a long arm and invited me inside.

The cabin had been built to accommodate Barry's massive height, so the living room I walked into had high ceilings with exposed wooden beams. Flames danced in the stone fireplace, and the planks of the wooden floor creaked softly beneath my feet.

"You have a beautiful home," I said.

"Thank you. Come on back to the greenhouse. You'll really like it there."

The back porch was walled in with glass, and it was filled with potted plants that Barry had brought in for the winter. Some of the plants even had fresh blooms on them, and I stopped to inhale deeply. The moist air had a soft, earthy scent.

"How much do you need?" Barry was moving toward a giant red pot jammed with borage. I wouldn't have been able to move it six inches, let alone carry it inside. For Barry, it had probably been a breeze.

"Marlee says the spell requires the leaves from two stalks."

"I'll give you double that, then." Barry laughed. "Just in case there's a mishap on the first try."

Coming from someone else, I might have been offended. Barry, I knew, was only gently teasing, so I laughed along with him. "I guess you've also heard gossip about the funeral home coven and our tendency to have magical misadventures."

"Chief Constable Hightower has told a tale or two."

"We've only rattled his windows a couple of times. Once, we set off a car alarm in a driveway two doors down. But, we're not dangerous or anything."

As a Bigfoot, Barry didn't exactly have eyebrows, but if he did, he would have been raising one in skepticism.

That night, Jo got home from the newspaper office just in time to eat a quick dinner, and then it was time to do the Happily Ever After spell. Marlee had been going over it for the past two hours, wanting to ensure her modifications were going to work.

We preferred doing our spell work outside, in the backyard. Being out in nature felt more appropriate when working magic. However, we were also middle-aged ladies who didn't enjoy being cold, wet, or uncomfortable. Since it was drizzling and windy outside, we opted to perform the spell in the kitchen, around the breakfast table.

That had the added benefit of allowing us to be seated, and I had to remind Marlee that there was no shame in being a lazy witch from time to time. Our familiars were taking it easy, too. Perkins had curled up in his nest with Marlee's toucan, Stella. Lonnie, Valerian's raven, had joined Gordon on the kitchen counter, and the two of them were watching the proceedings with interest.

While Marlee arranged everything we needed for the spell in a neat line on the table, Jo said hesitantly, "I have a confession. I did write an intention today. I thought about it all last night and today, and I am absolutely sure that whatever I manifest with this intention can't be anything bad."

"You mean, if it backfires—" I began.

"When," Valerian quipped.

"*If* it backfires," I repeated, "it will still be okay for you, Sam, Wanda, and anyone else involved with the newspaper drama?"

"Exactly." Jo's voice was self-assured. Then, in a softer tone, she added, "I think."

"Be confident," Marlee said. She lit a peach-colored pillar candle and slid it to the center of the table. "By doing this Happily Ever After spell, Jo, we're reinforcing the positive outcome of your intention. Val, can you please turn off the lights?"

Marlee slowly recited the words for the spell, motioning for all of us to join in when she began it a second time. On the third recitation, she picked up the stalks of borage and held them over the candle flame until the leaves began to give off a fragrant smoke. She moved the stalks in a circular motion around the candle, going clockwise three times, then set the bundle down in a metal bowl, where it continued to give off a sweet smell.

"Now," Marlee instructed, "join hands, and envision how everyone is connected and how a happily ever after for one of us is a happily ever after for all of us, including those who are not present with us tonight."

I closed my eyes and focused on everyone being happy, even Wanda. It wasn't easy, though.

Marlee brought the spell to a close, and Valerian turned the kitchen light on. "Wine?" Jo asked as she got up. "Or is it more of a hot chocolate night?"

We were evenly divided on the answer.

I had just opened the fridge, my eyes darting between the jug of milk and a bottle of chardonnay, when the doorbell rang.

"A visitor at this hour?" Jo's hand had frozen, halfway to reaching into the cabinet.

"Maybe it's Hazel's boyfriend."

"And maybe he's here to tell us the front door is wide open again." As soon as the words were out of my mouth, I realized what I'd done. "I mean," I stammered, "Wyatt is not my boyfriend."

I muttered to myself the entire walk to the front door, which was, in fact, closed and locked.

And it wasn't Wyatt standing on the porch when I opened the door. Instead, it was Nicole. Her hair was a bit messy, and she had some mascara smeared beneath her eyes.

"She's missing!" Nicole wailed. "I can't find Wanda!"

Chapter Seven

"When did you last see Wanda?" I asked as I took Nicole's hand and led her inside. I could feel her shaking.

"Um, just before I went out to eat dinner." Nicole tugged at the lapels of her coat, and her words came out in a tumble. "I stopped by her room at the hotel to ask if she needed anything. And she asked for some toothpaste, because she was out, but she said I could drop it by later, and when I went back, she wasn't there."

"Come sit down." I guided Nicole to the living room and pointed at the sofa. Then, I called down the hall, "Ladies! I need you!"

Not only did Valerian, Jo, and Marlee immediately come rushing down the hallway, but so did our familiars. They were all flying near the ceiling, and they ducked in a perfect line to get through the doorway into the living room.

"Nicole says Wanda is missing," I explained once we were all together.

Jo perched on the edge of the chair nearest Nicole. "How long has it been since you saw her?"

"A couple of hours, I think." Nicole sounded like she was on the verge of panicking, and Marlee quickly moved toward her and put a hand on her arm. Marlee knew exactly what Nicole was feeling, because she was feeling it, too, and she would be able to send soothing energy to help Nicole remain calm.

"You went back to Wanda's hotel room with the toothpaste?" I asked.

Nicole nodded.

"Maybe she was asleep, and she didn't hear you knocking."

"No. I have a key. I knocked, and when she didn't answer, I figured she was in the shower or something, so I let myself in. But no one was there."

"I hate to ask this," Jo said slowly, "but were there any signs of a struggle?"

"You think someone kidnapped her?" Nicole's voice rose in both pitch and volume with each word, and Marlee put her other hand on the woman's arm, too.

"These are the same questions the constables will ask," Jo said. "It's standard."

"Right. Right. Of course." Nicole shut her eyes briefly and took a deep breath. "I know I need to report it to them, but calling the constables means it's all real. It's scary. And Hazel is the only person in town who's been nice to me, and I don't want to do this by myself."

"You don't have to." I pulled my cell phone from the back pocket of my jeans. I knew I should be calling the constable station, but there was one constable who could get to the house faster than anyone else. I called Wyatt. When he picked up, I began with, "I'm so sorry to bother you, but someone has gone missing, and—"

"Are you at home?" Wyatt broke in.

"Yes."

"I'll be right there." He hung up, and I returned my attention to Nicole. The others were giving her as much assurance as they could, though, so I sat quietly and tried to collect my thoughts while we waited on Wyatt.

In just a few minutes, I heard footsteps pounding across the front porch, and then the sound of the door opening. I hadn't locked it when I'd ushered Nicole inside, and Wyatt wasn't going to wait for me to answer the doorbell. He appeared in the doorway of the living room, wearing a navy-blue sweater and blue jeans.

I hated bothering him when he was off-duty, but getting a lead on where Wanda might be seemed more important than interrupting Wyatt's evening.

Nicole repeated the information she'd already given us, and Wyatt asked the same question Jo had about any signs of a struggle. Before it could start to sound like déjà vu, though, Wyatt asked, "Does Wanda have any favorite spots around town?"

"We just got here, so I don't think she has any places she'd go to." I heard a *ding*, and then Nicole pulled her phone out of her pocket. She was staring at the screen, like she was reading a text message.

"Is it Wanda?" I asked.

Nicole shook her head and slid her phone back into her pocket. "No."

"Check the newspaper office," Jo suggested to Wyatt.

"It's the first place we're going to try." Wyatt looked at me. "We'll get a search underway, and I'm going to take Nicole with me to the constable station."

"Do you want me to go with you?" I asked Nicole.

Nicole stood slowly, then shook her head. "No. I'm feeling a lot calmer. Thank you, ladies."

Valerian looked at Wyatt. "Can we do anything to help?"

Wyatt hesitated, and when he glanced at me, I could see the uncertainty in his eyes. He seemed to have an inner debate, judging by the way his jaw clenched several times. Then, he said, "I'll take all the help I can get. Even magical help."

"We'll start right now," Valerian promised.

Wyatt quickly escorted Nicole out the front door and to his car. I was surprised he'd driven, considering he only lived three doors down, but he must have known he might have to head straight to the constable station. As the two of them went, I watched from the doorway. Wyatt was saying soothing things to Nicole, reassuring her that he and the other constables would do everything in their power to find Wanda. I'd never heard him speak so gently.

I felt a touch on my shoulder. "You're surprised about something," Marlee said.

I made a noncommittal noise. "This whole thing has been a surprise," I said. "I don't like Wanda, but I do hope they find her, safe and sound."

"I'm sure they will. Come on. Valerian is digging out her grimoire for a spell she's got for finding lost objects. Do you have any myrrh? It will help amplify the spell."

"Yeah, I'll go grab it." I watched Wyatt turn his car onto the street, then shut and locked the door.

The spell was so short and simple that it hardly felt like a spell. It only took us two minutes from the time we sat down at the breakfast table to the time we wrapped up. Even still, all four of us felt exhausted afterward. Spells took a lot of energy and magic, and doing two serious spells in one night was a strain.

None of us got up from our chairs at the conclusion of the spell. Jo declared she was too tired to even pour a glass of wine, and Marlee was yawning constantly.

"For once, I wish I had a buildup of excess magic. It would have come in handy tonight." I reached out and stroked the feathers along Perkins's back. He was sitting on the table, looking at me with concern.

None of us wanted to go to bed until we'd gotten an update on Wanda, despite how tired we were. So, instead of wine or hot chocolate, Valerian made us a pot of coffee. It helped us stay awake until my phone rang at seven minutes before midnight. It was Wyatt's name on the caller I.D.

"Wyatt?" I answered anxiously.

"False alarm," Wyatt said. Despite his reassuring tone, he sounded drained. "We found Ms. Whitcomb at her ex-husband's house."

That news woke me up more than the coffee had. "Wanda was hanging out with Aaron?"

Around me, I heard three shocked gasps.

"She was. I'm driving Nicole back to your house so she can get her rental car, but you don't need to stay up. She'll be heading straight to the hotel. That poor woman has had a long night."

"Thanks for your help, Wyatt."

"Just doing my job."

Despite the adventure on Monday night, Tuesday felt perfectly normal. I made three deliveries around town, got some work done on a hall closet I was trying to reorganize, and I even had time to curl up on the sofa with a book as the sun headed for the horizon.

Since Valerian and Jo were at work, it was just Marlee and me at home. In the mid-afternoon, Marlee was complaining of boredom, since she didn't have any immediate events to work on, so I finally suggested she tackle removing a patch of ugly mauve wallpaper that still clung stubbornly to one wall of the kitchen. At that, she quickly remembered she had a library book she needed to finish, so she grabbed a flannel blanket and joined me in the living room.

We were both enjoying our quiet reading when the front door opened, then slammed shut. Jo had a distinctive—and loud—footstep, but this was even more forceful than usual.

"Uh-oh," Marlee said under her breath, just before Jo appeared in the living room doorway, a livid look on her face.

"What happened?" I asked.

"Are you okay?" Marlee inquired at the same time.

"I can't believe we were worried about that woman last night!" Jo was shouting she was so angry. "She is absolutely relentless! Not only is she still hounding Sam, but she even had the nerve to come into my office to try to convince me that I should help her make this deal happen. She said she'd give me a new title if I did. Would it be editor? No, of course not! It would be senior staff writer. Seriously? Who does this woman think she is? I had to drive around for half an hour after I left work, just so I wouldn't start shouting as soon as I walked in the door."

Jo's hands had slowly curled into fists as she had been speaking, and after she fell silent, I saw the purple magic that shot out of her knuckles. Jo's buildup of magic either needed an outlet, or she needed to calm down, fast.

Marlee was already up out of her chair and heading for Jo. "We're going to the tavern. You need your entire coven with you, so we're going to Val. Plus, you could use the distraction. And a drink."

Jo held up her hands. "I'm okay. Well, I'm not, but let me shower and change. I need to calm down some before you take me anywhere."

Not only did Jo shower, but she also suggested we eat dinner, saying that food might further help her nerves. So, by the time we had eaten, cleaned up, and gotten ready to go, it was already a little past eight o'clock.

But Jo, clearly, still needed the magic of her coven. During dinner, she had muttered angrily in between every bite of her pasta.

We drove downtown in Marlee's compact SUV, but I was the one behind the wheel. Marlee and Jo sat in the back seat together, so Marlee could keep a hand clamped on Jo while she performed a calming spell.

When we walked inside the tavern, Jo paused, her head moving from side to side. She always seemed to be looking for someone when she walked into Sit a Spell Tavern, but whenever one of us asked her about it, she claimed she was just looking around.

Jo was still standing just inside the entrance when Ilya, the too-smiley man who'd said he was in town to see if he wanted to retire there, walked through the door and squeezed his way past Jo. "Did you hear?" he asked loudly. "They found Wanda Whitcomb."

"Yes, last night," I said. "She was just over at her ex's. Her phone must have been off."

"No, I mean they found her, just now, at the newspaper office." Ilya stabbed a finger in the direction of the street outside. "She's dead."

CHAPTER EIGHT

EVERYONE STANDING WITHIN HEARING distance of Ilya erupted into gasps, cries of shock, and even a few expletives.

There was such a commotion that Valerian came out from behind the bar to find out what had happened, and Ilya repeated what he'd just said.

Valerian narrowed her eyes at the man. "And how do you know that Wanda is dead?"

"I was on my way here, and when I walked past the newspaper office, the constables were just setting up the crime scene. I overheard a couple of them talking about what had happened."

Jo gave a choked cry, and she grabbed both Marlee's and my hands. "Did I do this? Is it my fault?"

"Of course not!" Valerian said firmly.

"You said your intention couldn't result in a bad outcome," I reminded Jo.

"I need to go look at it again. Maybe I missed something!"

"Before we take you home, I want to go look for Nicole. She was upset about not being able to locate

Wanda last night. Think what she must be feeling now that Wanda is dead."

Wanda is dead. It didn't seem real. The woman who seemed to be loathed by everyone she'd met in Foxfire Haven was dead, at the very place she had been trying to buy. I had a strong feeling it hadn't been a mere accident, or any kind of natural cause.

"Jo, you come sit down," Valerian instructed. "Was Wanda there when you left work today?"

"No. Sam managed to chase her off after lunch. If she died at the newspaper office, then it was sometime between when we all left around six o'clock and now." Jo looked at her watch. "That means it happened in the last two hours or so."

"Call Sam and find out what's going on," Valerian instructed, "while Marlee and Hazel go look for Nicole."

Marlee and I left, and since Wanda had died at the newspaper office, we headed straight there. It was just a short walk down Main Street, and like Ilya had said, the constables had set up crime scene tape and had officers standing guard to make sure no one could get into the small, two-story brick building.

Nicole was nowhere in sight. Neither was Sam, so I hoped Jo was having some luck getting him on the phone.

The only hotel in Foxfire Haven was the Traveler's Retreat, so Marlee and I headed there next. Like most places in the downtown area, it was a short walk, and it was on Main Street. The white three-story hotel was historic, like most of the buildings downtown, giving it an elegant, if slightly faded, look.

Unfortunately, when I asked the clerk at the counter for Nicole's room number, she told me that information was private. *Of course it is,* I chided myself. I had been so anxious to find Nicole I forgot hotels had policies in place to protect guests.

I considered loitering in the lobby until Nicole either left her room or returned to it, but that could be hours, and I didn't want to leave Jo hanging. So, feeling disappointed—and wishing I'd thought to ask Nicole for her phone number the night before—I trudged back to the tavern alongside Marlee.

Jo had her head down on the bar when we got back. Everyone else at the tavern was still buzzing with the news.

Marlee went right up to Jo and wrapped her arms around her from behind. "What's the word?"

Jo sat up. "Sam says our IT person went back to the office about forty-five minutes ago, because she wanted to update the publishing software on our computers after we were all gone for the day. She's the one who found Wanda."

"We had no luck finding Nicole," I told Jo. "So much for bringing you to the tavern for a drink and some time with your coven."

"I hope she's safe." Jo whispered it so quietly I could barely hear her, but it sent a spike of panic through me. If Wanda's death hadn't been accidental, had something happened to Nicole, too? I didn't know where to find her, and I had to trust that Wyatt and his constables were already trying to track her down. Maybe, I consoled myself, they already had.

"Hazel," Marlee said in a warning tone.

"What?"

Marlee was pointing toward my feet, and when I looked down, I saw some of my pink magic sparkling on the floor. "Great. Add a magical fart to today's adventures." I shook some magic off one foot. "We're heading home. Val, we'll see you when you get off work."

Valerian was already moving off to take the drink orders of four people who had just walked up to the bar. She was going to have a busy night. The tavern was known as the place to get town gossip, and as word spread about Wanda's death, more and more people would head to Sit a Spell to learn what they could.

And, if they couldn't learn anything, someone would probably make up something that sounded scandalous.

I drove home slowly, mindful that my magic had built up, and that any little surprise might trigger another embarrassing exhalation. If a bunny bounded out into the road in front of me, I was in danger of turning the entire interior of Marlee's car pink.

When we got home, Jo and Marlee went inside after Jo said she would get the intention she'd written about Wanda and meet us in the kitchen. I stayed in the backyard to do a quick controlled shed. *Two unexpected exhalations in just three days. I thought I was getting so much better.*

Jo was already sitting at the breakfast table, a paper spread out in front of her, when I came through the back door. Marlee was filling the tea kettle.

I watched as Jo's lips moved silently, and then she began to read out loud. "*Sam tells Wanda the newspaper is not for sale, and she realizes she doesn't really want it, anyway. She finds a better investment opportunity, one that will make both her and the seller happy. The opportunity will be in a magical town that is not Foxfire Haven. Sam and I will have a positive discussion about my future as editor of the* Foxfire Haven Recorder."

"You did not cause Wanda's death," I said confidently when Jo had finished.

"We knew that already," Marlee added, "but that intention was for Wanda to find a different business opportunity, not to die."

Jo sat back as her shoulders slumped. "I feel better."

We discussed Wanda's mysterious death while the tea brewed, but there just wasn't much to talk about. Until we heard details, there was no point in even speculating what might have happened. So, by the time Marlee had placed steaming cups of tea in front of each of us, we were ready to move on to other topics.

Jo had to scoot her chair back from the table to make space for Gordon, who insisted on sitting in her lap. The top of his head came up to Jo's chin, and she had to reach out awkwardly to get her cup of tea. Despite the grim situation, I had to smile at the comical scene before me. Pelicans were simply not lap animals, and I was glad my own familiar was so much more manageable.

In terms of size, at least. Perkins might have been small, but his personality was every bit as big as Gordon's.

The scene was much the same the next morning at breakfast, though Valerian had joined our glum-looking circle at the breakfast table, and we had swapped tea for coffee.

Despite the fact that none of us had liked Wanda, her death had still cast a pall over us. I was also still worried about Nicole, and I hoped we'd get word soon that she was safe.

I knew I wasn't the only one feeling that way when Jo said, "I didn't write about her assistant."

"I'm sure she's fine," Marlee said. She yawned, then added, "I did not sleep well."

"Me, neither." Valerian took a long sip of coffee. "I got home later than usual since the tavern was so busy, and even though I was exhausted, I couldn't stop thinking about this whole situation."

"We know Jo didn't do this with her manifesting," I said, "but did our spell somehow set off a chain of events?"

"Of course not," Valerian said quickly. "I don't think dying in the middle of a newspaper office counts as a happily ever after, so our spell certainly didn't have anything to do with Wanda's demise."

Despite all of us nodding our heads, not one of us really looked reassured. Even Valerian frowned into her coffee cup. After a long silence, she said quietly, "She came into the tavern for a late lunch yesterday. She was so demanding and rude! It was everything I could do not to slip that Mind Your Own Business potion into her soda."

"I saw her at the magic store," Marlee said. "She was telling the clerk how she'd feature the store in the newspaper, but only if they bought a big enough ad. The poor clerk kept saying she couldn't make those kinds of decisions, and that Wanda would have to talk to Adeline about it, but Wanda just wouldn't let up. I could feel that poor clerk's agitation."

"She bullied me about selling my house, and she clashed with Jo at the newspaper office." I shook my head. "We all had negative interactions with her, or saw her bullying others."

We lapsed into silence again. I was deep in thought about the fact that while our spell hadn't been a malicious one, our intentions might not have been as pure as they should have been. Had we accidentally killed Wanda by performing a spell without letting go of our negative feelings about her first? It felt like a long shot, but I knew it was a possibility.

It was the sound of the doorbell that finally broke me out of my dark thoughts. When I got to the door, I opened it expecting to find Wyatt standing there again, or maybe even Nicole.

Instead, I found myself looking at a man with close-cropped gray hair, pale skin that was shining from a layer of sweat, and wide, wild copper eyes. I had only met Sam Doane once, but I recognized him immediately.

"Sam, what's wrong?" I asked, reaching out to put a hand on one of his bony shoulders. I wasn't sure if I was doing it to reassure him or myself. He was breathing rapidly, and I was worried he might pass out right on my doorstep.

"Is Jo here?" Sam's voice was shaking.

"Of course. Come on. I'll get you some water, too. You don't look well."

"I'm not going to die anytime soon." Sam gave what I think was supposed to be a laugh, but it came out as more of a groan.

I insisted that Sam sit down in my vacated spot at the breakfast table. While I quickly poured a glass of water for him, he said sadly to Jo, "I came here to let you know that Wanda Whitcomb's death has been ruled a murder."

After all four of us sucked in our breath in unison, Sam added, "And I expect to be arrested as the prime suspect."

CHAPTER NINE

JO JUMPED FROM THE shock of Sam's announcement, sending Gordon flying off her lap. One of his giant wings caught the handle of her coffee cup, and its contents spilled out as the cup went skittering across the table. Marlee yelped, Valerian shouted something incoherent, and Lonnie the raven, who was perched on the windowsill, let out a cackling caw.

By the time Gordon had flown out the back window, a few coffee-soaked feathers were strewn across the table, and Marlee was using one half of her bagel to sop up coffee before it could drip down onto the floor.

I grabbed a towel and joined the fight, and once I saw we had things relatively under control, I returned my attention to Sam. "Why do the constables think Wanda was murdered?"

"Because she was found with my favorite fountain pen in her jugular," Sam said. He sighed. "I only use it for signing my name to things, but I'd always called it my lucky pen. Guess it's out of both ink and luck now."

"Even if it was your pen," Valerian said, "that doesn't mean the constables are going to arrest you for her murder."

“I agree. Unfortunately, I wrote an opinion piece about Wanda that ran in today’s edition. I wasn’t kind to her in it.”

“I read it this morning,” Jo said. As if to prove it, she lifted a section of the newspaper from where it had been sitting on the table. Coffee trickled from one corner of the soggy paper.

“I’m going to need you, Jo.”

“What can I do?”

“If I get arrested, you have to run things while I’m in jail.”

Jo’s eyes widened, and she pressed her lips together, but she didn’t respond.

“I know you can handle it,” Sam said firmly.

“You want me to take over as editor?” Jo asked, her voice barely above a whisper. Then, in a louder voice, she added, “If you get arrested, I mean.”

Sam nodded. “You know the operation almost as well as I do. I wouldn’t trust anyone else to be interim editor.”

Jo swallowed so hard I thought I actually heard it. Instead of looking honored by the task, she looked terrified. Still, she gave Sam a firm nod. “You can count on me.”

“But I’m sure it won’t come to that,” Valerian broke in. “You wouldn’t be stupid enough to write a scathing opinion piece, then kill her with your favorite pen. It’s more likely someone is trying to set you up.”

“Not that many people knew about the piece before it was published,” Sam pointed out. “I expect the timing is just a coincidence, as was the murder weapon. Who in this town would want to frame me for murder? Though I do appreciate knowing you’re on my side, Val.”

"We're all behind you," Marlee said firmly.

"Thanks, ladies." Sam looked slightly less ashen and wide-eyed than he had when I'd opened the front door for him. "I need to get to the office. Jo, I'll see you in a bit. The rest of you, enjoy your morning."

Jo walked Sam out, and I turned to Marlee and Valerian. "How are we supposed to enjoy our morning after news like that?"

Neither one of them had an answer.

When Jo came back into the kitchen, her shoulders were slumped, and she was pulling on the ends of two of her braids. "My intention did not cause this," she said, repeating it like a mantra.

"No, it did not," Valerian said, catching Jo's hand and pulling it gently away from her hair. "Neither did our spell. Someone disliked Wanda much more than we did, and that's that."

"You're right. Of course. I'm just worried that this is how I get to be editor, and it's my fault for setting that career goal." Jo sat down, sighed, then stood up again. "I need to get to the office. Ugh. My workplace isn't just reporting the news. We *are* the news."

We offered words of encouragement as Jo trudged out the door and down the hall toward her room. Marlee also told her to meet the rest of us at the garden store that night for our second plant magic class. "It will be good for you," Marlee insisted.

Valerian had the day off, and she and Marlee were planning to drive to Stanton to visit an antique mall there. They had asked me to join them, but I had something more important on my agenda.

At promptly ten o'clock that morning, my phone dinged, alerting me that I had an incoming video call. It was my daughter, Tara, and soon, I was looking at her face through the screen. The older she got, the more she looked like me. Or, at least, the way I had looked when I had been in my late twenties. Her gray eyes and blond hair reminded me of myself when I had been half the age I was now.

"Hey, honey," I said.

"Hi, Mom." Tara smiled warmly at me, and I felt a sense of calm wash over me. Her affection was exactly what I needed after the morning we'd had. Things were getting better between Tara and me, after a tense few months following the magical exhalation I'd had at my granddaughter's dance recital.

"Is Hailey getting along better with the other kids at pre-school?" I asked.

Tara laughed. "She pitched a fit when I told her she wasn't going in until after lunch today. She said I was getting in the way of her being a pirate on the playground. Luckily, once I told her it was because she had a lesson with you, she calmed down considerably."

That news made me feel even better. Witchcraft had skipped a generation with Tara, but Hailey had it in full force. She was a precocious three-year-old, and teaching her to control her growing abilities was a task not just for me but my entire coven. Hailey and I had weekly one-on-one video calls, so I could keep track of how she was progressing.

"How's it going with the herb garden?" I asked. For Christmas, I had given Hailey a tiny herb garden designed for growing indoors. The tray full of dirt was divided into six sections, so a variety of herbs could be grown.

"Well, the dog ate the basil." Tara's mouth twisted into a grimace. "Otherwise, it's all growing nicely. I made tea with the mint, and it was really good."

I heard several loud clunks, followed by "Gamma!" A moment later, Hailey's face appeared on my phone screen. "Guess what?"

"What, Hailey?"

"I'm a pirate."

"I heard. Are you the captain of the ship, or do you make people walk the plank?"

"I cook." Hailey stuck her chin out proudly. "I cook cheese and crackers."

"Well done. How does your magic feel when you're a pirate?"

Hailey looked thoughtful, her lips poking out. "It feels good. I'm a witch pirate."

"Yes, you are. I'm glad your magic stays under control when you're playing with your friends." I knew all too well how a stressful situation could cause a magical outburst, and I figured the role of ship's cook was a good, low-key choice for Hailey.

"Can we sing that song again?"

I'd come up with a simple song about learning to recognize when our magic was growing stronger. Marlee had caught me singing it absently while loading the dishwasher one night, and I had recently heard her humming the tune. It was catchy.

Hailey and I sang the song together, and then we proceeded with our lesson. After Hailey's own magical exhalation at preschool, Tara had asked me for help, and since then, Hailey had made a lot of progress in sensing when she was, as she put it, "filling up with magic stuff."

I'd invited Tara, her husband, and Hailey up for Christmas, and we'd made a lot of progress because Hailey and I had been in the same place. Plus, she had gotten to work with the entire coven. Being around other witches was really good for her own development.

Even still, I didn't want to move back to San Francisco. I was happy in Foxfire Haven, and I knew it would be dangerous for me to go back to the mundane world when I was still learning to rein in my magic. And, since both Tara and her husband, Brian, had good jobs where they were, they had no interest in moving to Foxfire Haven.

So, instead, we stuck to video calls once a week, and sometimes more if Hailey was having a particularly hard time with her magic, or when there was something special to celebrate, like a lunar eclipse.

Nearly an hour had passed by the time Hailey started yawning and blinking her eyes. I told her she'd done a good job, said goodbye to Tara, then hung up, stifling my own yawn.

Marlee and Valerian got home from Stanton just in time for lunch. Marlee walked into the kitchen triumphantly, waving a tiara over her head. It was at least six inches tall, with rhinestones that glittered in the overhead lights.

"Are you going to give up being a witch to become a princess?" I inquired.

"Why can't I be both?" Marlee asked seriously.

I shrugged and grabbed a loaf of bread so I could make sandwiches for all of us. "Good point. Hailey has informed me that she's now a witch pirate."

"That's a great career choice," Valerian said with an approving nod.

"Sadly, the tiara is not for me," Marlee said, a bit wistfully. "I thought I'd add it to my stash of supplies for bachelorette parties and wedding showers. That way, the bride-to-be can feel like a princess without having to buy her own tiara."

By the time we sat down to lunch, Valerian had gone into a detailed account of her own wedding shower, which had included the maid of honor confessing she was in love with one of the groomsmen, a pet snake getting lost among the pile of presents, and a pot of tea that was spelled to taste like the drinker's favorite wine.

My own, non-magical wedding shower had been downright boring in comparison.

I was just putting our plates into the dishwasher when Wyatt called. I made the mistake of announcing that before I answered, and I swatted at Marlee and Valerian as they both batted their eyelashes and chorused, "Ooh!" No matter how hard I tried, I couldn't get them to stop teasing me about the man who was the very opposite of my boyfriend.

"Maybe you'll be needing this soon!" Marlee said, waving the tiara in my direction.

"Ugh" was my only response. Unfortunately, I said it right as I answered Wyatt's call.

"You're that happy to hear from me, huh?" he intoned.

"No, sorry. That was for Marlee. Hello, Wyatt."

"I'm heading home for a late lunch. Do you mind if I stop by your place?"

"Not at all. We'll be here."

Wyatt refused to tell me what the reason for the visit was, so that left us with time to speculate as we waited for him to arrive.

When Wyatt knocked at the door about fifteen minutes after I'd hung up the phone, Marlee and Valerian quickly disappeared into their rooms, assuming Wyatt wanted his conversation with me to be private.

Unfortunately, when I opened the door, I was interrupted before I could so much as say hello.

Holman materialized right beside me, a smug smile underneath his pencil-thin mustache. "Hello, Chief Constable Hightower."

Wyatt gaped at the ghost. Even living in a magical town couldn't prepare anyone for the surprise that was Holman. Wyatt recovered quickly and said, "Hello. You're the former director here, right?"

"Yes. And I just wanted to say that your hair looks very nice. I've never understood why men feel the need to color their hair when it begins to turn gray." Holman patted his blond waves. "I certainly never had a need to do so. Anyway, Marlee says I should show up to give compliments once in a while, so that's what I'm doing."

Holman's lips pressed together, and he turned slowly toward me with a pained expression. Clearly, there was more he wanted to say.

"Out with it, Holman." Otherwise, I knew, there would be no peace.

"It's that uniform!" Holman exclaimed. He turned back to Wyatt and began to gesture wildly. "First of all, that shade of gray is doing nothing for your skin tone or those sparkling eyes. Second, the cut of the shirt is just horrid. So boxy! A tailored shirt would show off your excellent physique better."

I looked at Wyatt, embarrassed by Holman's outburst, but he was snickering.

"Thank you, Holman. That's the first time a ghost has complimented my looks."

"Not the message I was trying to send. Do something about that uniform, and women will be confessing crimes to you just so they can gaze into those blue eyes."

"I'll take that interrogation tactic under consideration."

Holman turned to me. "See, Hazel? I said something nice." Before I could argue that one nice compliment hardly outweighed his criticisms, he disappeared.

"Sorry," I told Wyatt.

"Honestly, that was the highlight of my day. Anyway, I'm here because I understand Nicole Murrow's visit here Monday night wasn't her first."

"That's correct. Is she doing all right? I mean, considering Wanda's murder."

"She's hanging in there, but I need you to tell me everything about your conversations with her."

"Why?"

In answer, Wyatt just lifted an eyebrow. He didn't need to tell me what he was thinking, because I could read it clearly in his expression. Wyatt thought Nicole might have snapped and killed her boss.

Chapter Ten

"She couldn't have," I blurted.

Wyatt's eyebrow had started to settle down, but it shot up again. "Couldn't have, what?"

"There is no way Nicole killed Wanda. Right? She seemed nice enough, and she was so upset the night Wanda went missing."

"I expect she was both nice and worried, but we all thought Petunia over at Growing Power Garden Store was nice, too," Wyatt noted.

He had a good point. Petunia had been nice to me, but she hadn't been so nice when she'd killed someone.

"Plus," he added, "did you know that after we located Ms. Whitcomb at her ex-husband's home, she yelled at Ms. Murrow for involving the constables? She even threatened to fire her."

"I didn't know that." I waved Wyatt inside. "Come on in. I made sandwiches for lunch. You want me to make you one?"

Wyatt seemed surprised by my offer of lunch. Frankly, so was I.

"You said you were heading home for a late lunch," I pointed out when he didn't respond.

"Thanks, but this is just a business visit."

I led Wyatt into the kitchen, anyway, then filled the kettle and put teabags into two cups so I could at least offer him a cup of tea. Once I had the kettle heating up, I joined Wyatt at the breakfast table. He had already settled into a chair there, and he was gently stroking Perkins on the back with one finger.

"So, if you know Nicole got yelled at on Monday night, then you must have questioned her already," I said.

"We did talk to her, but she didn't tell us about that incident. All the witnesses did."

"Ah, I see. Wanda humiliated Nicole in front of a crowd."

Wyatt nodded. Even if Nicole hadn't raised suspicion when the constables had spoken to her, I could see how a public showdown like that might give them pause. If Wanda had threatened to fire Nicole simply for being worried about her, then what other horrible ways had she treated her assistant in the past? Maybe Nicole really had snapped. Perhaps this latest embarrassment was the last in a long line of them, and she'd used Sam's fountain pen to make sure Wanda could never humiliate her again.

I shuddered at the idea. "I met her Sunday evening, when I pulled up to the house and found her standing on the porch," I began. "Wanda had seen this place and decided it might be grand enough for her tastes, so she sent Nicole to ask me how much I wanted for it."

"I remember you telling me that, but what else did she say during that conversation? Did she say anything about her work, or anything specific about Wanda?"

"She mentioned Wanda having a phrase she liked to use, about how everything is for sale, and it's just a matter of negotiation. I got the impression that Wanda is a bit of a pushy woman. Or was, anyway. Of course, I was right."

"What do you mean?"

The kettle began to whistle, so I got up and poured the boiling water into the cups. As the tea steeped, I stared into the steaming liquid. "I ran into Wanda at Stacy's shop. It did not go well." I proceeded to tell Wyatt how Wanda had me backed up against a display of cards, and how I'd had to stand firm about not selling my home.

By the time I'd finished, the tea was ready, so I took the teabags out and turned to Wyatt. "Do you take one spoonful of sugar with your tea, just like you drink your coffee?"

"I do, thank you."

I could sense Wyatt's hesitation as I placed his cup in front of him. Even Perkins was looking at him dubiously, his head tilted sideways.

"Hazel," Wyatt said, slowly turning his cup, "you know I have my doubts about your ability to control your magic."

I made a dismissive noise. "I'm doing much better!" Even as I said it, though, I caught sight of a faint pink glow around my fingertips. I quickly dropped my hands off the table and shook them as discreetly as I could, trying to fling off the excess magic.

Why does he get me so worked up?

Thankfully, Wyatt hadn't seemed to notice, probably because he was still staring down at his teacup rather than looking at me or my wayward magic. Finally, he looked up at me. "Despite my reservations about your control, I meant what I said to you back before Christmas. Your style of magic is rooted in your strong intuition, and the way you draw information to yourself without even realizing it. You said yourself that clues seem to present themselves to you, but what really counts is that you recognize them as clues. Other people probably hear the same bits of conversation, or encounter similar situations with suspects, but you're the one who's able to sort the clues from the clutter."

"Are you asking for my help with this murder investigation?" I asked tentatively.

"Not in an official capacity, no. But please keep an eye out, and call me with news that might seem relevant. Don't dismiss anything that might pertain to this case."

I breathed in deeply, feeling pride blooming in my chest. Wyatt had just paid me a huge compliment by asking me to help him, even if it was in an unofficial way. My spine and chin both lifted. "I'm happy to pass along anything that seems related." I was trying, and failing, to keep the excitement out of my voice.

"And I'd like you to especially keep an eye on Ms. Davenport. Everyone knows she wants to be editor and publisher of the *Foxfire Haven Recorder* someday."

I felt like a balloon that had just been stabbed with a pin. Or, perhaps, like a Wanda that had just been stabbed with a pen. All the pride and excitement fled, leaving me deflated.

Deflated and angry.

"You want me to spy on my friend and my roommate," I said flatly. "Jo is a member of my coven."

"Which puts you in an advantageous position to monitor her."

I stood abruptly, the chair legs squealing against the wooden floor. "Jo didn't kill anyone, and I am not going to spy on her!"

"But, Hazel—"

"No. Absolutely not."

Wyatt opened his mouth, then wisely shut it. "Fine. Don't help me, then." He rose and stalked out of the kitchen. A few seconds later, I heard the front door open and close.

"You stupid, mean old man!" I shouted at the empty kitchen. A heavy concentration of magic puffed out from my body, like a glittery pink marshmallow. I let out a guttural yell in my frustration, which brought Marlee and Valerian running into the kitchen.

"Oh!" Marlee reached a hand toward me. "So much magic! What did Wyatt do to you?"

I could only sputter in answer. Marlee stepped toward me, waving her hands to clear the air a bit, and looked at me closely. "You are feeling so many things right now."

"So many," I agreed. I gave myself a shake, and some more magic puffed out of my body. "He asked me to keep an eye on Jo, in case she was involved in Wanda's murder."

Valerian made a low growling noise, like a wild animal. "He said that?"

"Not the part about Jo being involved in the murder, but he did ask me to keep close watch on her in case I learned anything relevant that could help the investigation."

Marlee very unexpectedly began to giggle. "And you got rid of him for asking such an awful thing of you. Good! I'm proud of you!"

I went outside to do a spell that helped shed my magic. Not surprisingly, even more was extracted from me during the process, but it just trickled down into the soil and grass below me. And, even though my magic was back to a normal level, I was still upset Wyatt had asked me to turn informant on someone in my own coven. Not knowing what else to do, I channeled all that energy into cleaning the basement. I was rewarded for it with a stiff, sore back by the end of the afternoon, plus a scratch on my arm from the surprisingly sharp edge of an old metal sign that read *Funeral Today*. I kept the sign, though. It was a pretty cool vintage piece.

By the time Marlee, Valerian, and I drove to our plant magic class that night, I was feeling better. Valerian wasn't even enrolled in the class, but she'd had so much fun as a guest instructor that she figured she'd go back again. She knew Gnorris would welcome having her help.

The three of us were already stationed at a table, a potted lemon verbena in front of each of us, when Jo came in, looking harried.

"You okay?" Marlee asked instantly.

"Sam hasn't been arrested, so yeah, I'm okay. It was just a busy day, since our office is the top gossip in Foxfire Haven, and it felt like half the town stopped in on some kind of made-up business so they could feel like they were part of the drama."

After Gnorris gave us a short introduction to lemon verbena, he set us to work trimming back the ones in front of us. "If they're not pruned properly, they'll get too unwieldy to raise indoors," he had told us. "But if you trim too erratically, they'll die. It's a delicate balance."

Jo was so focused on doing a good job of pruning her plant that she was absolutely silent. The distraction was probably exactly what she needed after her eventful day at work.

In fact, it was my turn to mangle a plant, like Jo had done at Sunday evening's class. I was snipping a leaf when I felt a small hand against my elbow, and I looked down to see Gnorris shaking his head.

"Hazel, it's going to be dead before class ends if you keep treating it like that."

That got Jo to look up from her own plant. "Yikes. What's with you? Did something happen?"

"Don't get her started!" Valerian warned.

"And, whatever you do," Marlee added, "do not bring up the subject of the Foxfire Haven Constables."

Jo smirked at me. "Clashing with Chief Constable Hightower again?"

"He's just. Such. A. Stupid—" I was clacking my pruning shears with each word, and Gnorris touched my elbow again. This time, though, he got a good grip and guided my arm back, away from the plant.

"I think you should put those down," he said. "Everyone in town is talking about the murder of that woman from Florida, but you're murdering that plant, right in front of all these witnesses."

I looked down at my lemon verbena. "Sorry, Gnorris. I'll be gentler with it." To prove I was serious, I put the pruning shears down on the table and gave one of the leaves a gentle pat. "Sorry, plant."

After Gnorris had moved off, satisfied I wasn't going to continue taking out my frustrations on my plant, I quietly told Jo about Wyatt's request that I keep an eye on her.

To my surprise, she shrugged it off. "He's right to keep an eye on me. Wanda was after the newspaper, I'm a longtime employee there, and I've got a vested interest in its future. But I do agree with you that it was tacky to ask you to spy on me. That goes against everything a coven stands for."

After class, the four of us lingered as the other students drifted out. Jo said she had some follow-up questions for the story she was writing about the class, and I wanted to apologize to Gnorris again.

Before either Jo or I could talk to him, though, the front door of the shop banged open, and a woman rushed through it. She stopped short in front of Gnorris, patted the thick black bun on top of her head, and tugged on the hem of her forest-green coat. "Whew. I'm so glad you're still open. I need a rosebush for a Lay it to Rest spell."

Gnorris was craning his neck up to look at the woman, and she squatted down so they would be on the same level. Her dark skin and high, elegant cheekbones made her a sharp contrast to the gnome's rosy cheeks set in a pale, very round face, and I thought of a bedtime story from my childhood about a fairy queen and a gnome king who made an alliance together.

"A Lay it to Rest spell?" Gnorris asked dubiously. "I'm no witch, but I do know that you should use an anemone plant instead. It's far more effective."

The woman shook her head. “He insists on roses. He says a rosebush will look good in the yard, and the spell will help him process his grief faster since his ex-wife was murdered last night.”

Chapter Eleven

I HAD BEEN WATCHING Gnorris and the newcomer, casually waiting for my turn to talk to him, but at the woman's words, I pointedly looked anywhere but at them. I wanted to eavesdrop, but I didn't want to look like I was eavesdropping.

Which, of course, probably meant I was being very obvious about it. So, when Gnorris moved off to retrieve the plant the woman had asked for, I took a step toward her as she straightened back up. "I met Aaron recently," I told her. "I'm sorry for his loss."

Is it really a loss for him, though? He was so upset about Wanda showing up in Foxfire Haven.

The woman seemed to agree with my unspoken sentiment. "Between you and me, I don't think he's grieving all that much. He just wants closure, and this spell will help. Aaron wants to move on."

I smiled sympathetically. "I can't imagine what I would do if my ex showed up in town. And if he told me he was moving here to take over a business? I'd probably hide in my attic and never come out. Anyway, I hope the spell works for Aaron. How long have you two been together?"

The woman laughed heartily. "I'm not his wife. I'm his business partner! We started our accounting and financial consulting firm eight years ago." She fished a business card out of her purse and handed it to me. "Lenox Williams. Keep me in mind if you ever need financial services."

"I will, thanks." I glanced at the card, then slid it into the front pocket of my jeans. "Did you ever meet Wanda?"

"Only once or twice, years ago. Aaron and I started our business down in Osbourne, and he was going through his divorce while we were getting things off the ground. He tried to keep his work life and his personal life separate, but I've heard the stories in the years since. If you ask me, the newspaper dodged a bullet. If she's half as controlling of her businesses as she was her husband—"

Lenox cut off as Gnorris came back. The anemone he was carrying was nearly as big as he was, and I instinctively bent down and plucked it from his arms. I set it on the countertop while Lenox got her wallet out to pay for it. I had hoped she might stick around, but she gave me an apologetic nod. "I need to get this to Aaron so he can do the spell tonight. It was nice meeting you..."

"Hazel," I supplied.

"Hazel. Oh! Underwood, right?" Lenox looked around at the four of us. "The funeral home coven, of course. Hey, Val, I didn't even see you there. Best bartender in town! Have a good night, witches!" With that, Lenox was gone, disappearing through the door almost as quickly as she'd entered it.

"I was hoping to ask her about Wanda's little field trip to Aaron's house," I muttered.

Marlee giggled. "I think that's what the constables are for."

"I thought we weren't supposed to be talking about them?" Jo asked, looking at me wickedly.

"I'm okay, as long as there aren't any pruning shears around." I smiled. "Let's go home, where we can get away from talk of the murder."

Except, when we got home, we continued to discuss Wanda's demise. As we sat in the breakfast nook with our familiars and steaming mugs of hot cocoa, we talked about who might have disliked Wanda enough to kill her. Nicole, we knew, was already on the suspect list as far as Wyatt was concerned.

"What about her ex-husband?" Marlee mused. "You heard what his business partner said tonight. He's not really that grief-stricken."

"And he claimed to be so unhappy she was in town, yet she was at his house on Monday night," Valerian added. "If my ex showed up like that, I would have let him stand outside in the cold and rain. No way would I let him into my home."

"I do appreciate Lenox dropping that tidbit about Aaron wanting to move on, and quick," I said. "I just wish I could have talked to her more. Aaron's hurry to move on is something I should let Wyatt know about, and more details would have been helpful."

We all agreed that Nicole and Aaron were looking like the top suspects in the case. Jo said she and Sam were on the list, too, but the two of them seemed like long shots compared to those whose lives were so much more connected to Wanda's.

Finally, once the last of my cocoa was gone, I sighed. "I'm going to bed. The sooner I fall asleep, the sooner I can stop thinking about what I'm going to say to Wyatt tomorrow morning."

"Is calling Wyatt really that bad?" Valerian was peering at me. "You're not going to apologize for kicking him out, are you?"

"No! But I am going to tell him about Aaron's Lay it to Rest spell."

"So, if we hear crashing noises in the kitchen tomorrow morning," Marlee teased, "we'll know it's just you after talking to Wyatt."

"I promise not to break anything."

I drank two cups of coffee on Thursday morning, picked up my phone, then decided I could use a third cup. By the time I was done with that, I was downright jittery. So, naturally, I decided I needed to wait until the caffeine racing through my system had calmed down a bit before I called Wyatt.

Really, I was just putting it off. I wanted to tell him about my conversation with Lenox the night before, but at the same time, I wasn't looking forward to talking to a man I was still angry with.

What finally convinced me to get it over with was a text from Jo. She had gotten to the office about half an hour before, and she sent a text to the entire coven to say we might need to do another spell that night. This time, it wouldn't be for happily ever afters, but to get people to mind their own business. *People are treating all of us on staff like suspects,* Jo had typed. *It's gone from curiosity to rudeness.*

My heart broke for Jo that she was having to endure such treatment by town busybodies. So, with her in mind—as well as Sam—I steeled myself and called Wyatt.

He sounded wary when he answered, managing to turn a single "hello" into something that conveyed trepidation and weariness.

"I was just calling to pass on some information." I didn't mention our disagreement, or the way he'd stomped out of my house the day before, leaving his cup of tea untouched. Quickly, I relayed my discussion with Lenox, told him to have a good day, and hung up before he could so much as say thank you. I figured that was the safest way to keep the peace.

Valerian had left early for work, saying she wanted to swing by the library before her midday shift started. Marlee was at the supermarket, and Jo was at work. That meant I had the house to myself, and since I didn't have any deliveries to make that morning, I seriously considered using the free time to sprawl on the couch with a book and a fluffy blanket.

Instead, though, I settled in behind the walnut desk in the small office off the front hallway. The desk was ridiculously large, and it dominated the room. One of the former funeral directors had installed it, and I didn't have any inclination to get rid of it. I wasn't even sure it would fit through the door.

My laptop seemed tiny on the desk, but at least I had plenty of space for laying out the bills I needed to pay. I had just paid the repair bill for the washing machine—the clunky old thing had sputtered out just before Christmas—when I caught movement in my peripheral vision.

I turned my head to the right to see a cigar box full of old receipts flying across the room. It had been sitting on a bookcase against one wall, and it sailed more than the width of the desk before banging into a small table.

There was absolutely no way the box had fallen. It had been thrown. And, since Holman wasn't able to manipulate physical objects, that meant there was, without a doubt, a second ghost haunting our home. The front door opening by itself wasn't something I could keep blaming on bad locks or the door not sitting right in the frame. A ghost was opening the door, and now, it had thrown something across my office.

"Hello?" I said to the air.

There was no answer, unless the goosebumps that crawled up my arms counted as one.

I snatched up my laptop and made a hasty retreat to the kitchen. It wasn't like I would be safe from a ghost just by moving to a different room, but the atmosphere in there felt lighter. Plus, it was literally lighter: there were no windows in the office, so the kitchen windows and a peek at the world outside made me feel less trapped.

I was still sitting at the breakfast table, my laptop open but my mind focused on everything I'd ever learned about ghosts, when I heard the squeak of the front door opening.

Great. The ghost is at it again.

Except, it was Marlee, home from the supermarket. She came into the kitchen with three canvas shopping bags: one over her shoulder, one in each hand, and all of them nearly overflowing.

I laughed, my discomfort dissolving now that I wasn't home alone. "Are we hosting a dinner party?"

"No, I'm just stocking up to get through the weekend, but I am throwing a party! I just got hired to coordinate a memorial party for Wanda Whitcomb."

I wrinkled my nose. "Most of this town didn't even know her. Those who did know her didn't like her, including us. Nicole must have been loyal to the end—and beyond—if she hired you to throw Wanda a memorial party, despite everything."

Marlee heaved the shopping bags onto the countertop. "Oh, no, she's not the one throwing the party. Sam Doane is putting it on, and he called me himself to make the arrangements."

Chapter Twelve

I REPEATED MARLEE'S NEWS back to her, thinking I must have misheard her. "You're telling me that Sam, who wrote a scathing opinion piece about Wanda and figures he's suspect number one in her murder, is throwing a shindig to commemorate her?"

"You are correct." Marlee nodded as she began to pull items out of one of the shopping bags. "I know. It's bonkers, right? But I have a theory: I think Sam is doing this to make himself look like less of a suspect."

"Or he wants to ease his conscience," I mused.

"At any rate, it's welcome work in my slow season! Are you available for some delivery runs for the party?"

"Of course! When is this, er, *party*, anyway?" It seemed strange to call it a party when it was for a dead woman, but then again, I had always appreciated the term *celebration of life*, so maybe this wasn't all that different.

Marlee opened the fridge and deposited a few items inside it. "Saturday night."

I knew I must have misheard her that time. "That's in two days."

Marlee straightened up. “I know. It’s not ideal, for me or for you. You’re about to be really busy. But think of the extra money!”

She had a good point, and I said as much.

“Sam is even paying my rush fee,” Marlee continued. “This will really help tide me over until we get into peak wedding season.”

“Here, let me help you.” I got up and started putting some of the groceries away. “By the way, I had a little paranormal adventure in my office about half an hour ago. I watched a cigar box fly across the room.”

In response, Marlee sighed deeply. “We have another ghost here. I know.”

I blinked slowly at Marlee. “You know? How?” She had been the last of us to meet Holman, and if she had encountered another ghost, I would have expected her to pipe up about it.

Marlee put down a cabbage and twisted her hands together. “Something similar happened in my room a few weeks ago. I had a stack of laundry that was folded, but I hadn’t put it away yet. All of a sudden, it was like the clothes just exploded. There were T-shirts and underwear halfway across my bedroom.”

“Some supernatural force sent your clothes flying.”

“Yeah. I didn’t say anything because we were in the middle of the holidays, and I didn’t want to bring down the mood. Your daughter and her family were here, and everything was so festive. Then, since it didn’t happen again, I guess I sort of forgot about it.”

No wonder Marlee hadn’t wanted to point out the ghostly activity when it had first happened. My daughter was wary enough about witchcraft, so I could only imagine what she would have thought about being in a haunted house. Even Holman had politely steered clear of her.

We often found photos Uncle Grant had taken, and sometimes, photos he was in. A while back, Marlee had found a photo of a row of caskets in the showroom. There had been a bearded man in the photo who was definitely not Uncle Grant. And, on closer inspection, we realized the man was transparent. Was the ghost in that photo the same one who had flung the cigar box across the room?

At the moment, though, there was no way of knowing, and Marlee was already getting back to the subject of the party. She planned to spend the afternoon pinning down a venue for the event.

I, on the other hand, had a delivery to make. A young werewolf, fresh out of college, had just moved to Foxfire Haven for a job. He needed help getting some furniture from the store to his new apartment. When he'd called, I'd told him I wouldn't be able to haul heavy furniture up any stairs. He'd laughed and assured me the lifting part was no problem since werewolves had incredible strength. Getting everything home from the store was his issue, since he rode a motorcycle.

The young man's name was Charles, and I picked him up so we could go to the furniture store together. That way, he could help me do the heavy lifting on both ends of the operation. Charles had known I used a hearse for deliveries, but he still looked wowed when I pulled up in front of the apartment complex. Before we left for the store, he insisted on taking photos of my hearse and his motorcycle together.

The furniture barely fit into the back of the hearse, and the only thing that kept it all from overflowing was the fact that most of it required assembly. I figured Charles had a long evening with a screwdriver and an Allen wrench ahead of him, but we easily got everything out of the hearse and into his apartment.

Once that was wrapped up, I was on my way home when I spotted Nicole. She was standing on the sidewalk near the newspaper office. At first, I couldn't tell who she was talking to, but as I continued to drive, I saw it was none other than Ilya. He had a hand on one of Nicole's shoulders, and he was leaning his head toward her intently.

I wanted to stop to give Nicole my condolences, and to see how she was holding up, but she and Ilya seemed to be having a serious conversation. The odd retirement-town hunter must have been giving her his own condolences, I decided. Even still, something about Ilya put me on alert. I didn't quite buy his excuse for being in town, but at the same time, he hadn't said or done anything to make me think he was a bad guy.

"But he did show up in town at the same time as Wanda," I mumbled to myself. *Strange.*

When I got home, I was still wondering if Ilya had some kind of connection to Wanda, but my thoughts were interrupted by a call from Jo.

She was calling to complain. "It's swung the other way," she moaned. "I had thought I preferred the curious people to the rude people, but I take it back! I'd rather be accused of murder by another bored retiree than have someone taking pictures of me working. They say it's for social media, so they can document the murder investigation. Sam has started locking the front door, but they still find a way in!"

"Everyone is a true crime enthusiast these days," I said wryly. "Why don't you work from home? I promise, I won't take your photo."

"I can't. Sam and I have a meeting. Hazel, I think this is it. I think Sam is going to talk to me about my future with the newspaper. Can you and the other gals do a little magic to boost my chances?"

"Coming right up," I promised. I wished Jo luck, then found Marlee in the dining room. She was happily drawing a line through something written on the yellow legal pad in front of her. "Venue booked!" she announced. "By some miracle, the community center is free Saturday night."

"Great! Can you take a break to do some magic for Jo?"

I hadn't even finished explaining Jo's request before Marlee was on her feet. "Let's go to the tavern. Val should have a few minutes to help us do a spell. It will be more effective with three of us instead of just two."

"Maybe the familiars can come along, too. I'll go let them know the plan."

I found all four of our familiars sitting in a line on a branch of the bare maple tree in the front yard, looking out at the street like winged sentinels. "Hello!" I called to them. "We're going to the tavern to do a spell for Jo. She wants a boost in getting the career she wants. Would all of you like to help?"

Gordon's giant beak bobbed up and down. Of course he wanted to help his witch.

"If you're up for it, we'll meet you at the tavern."

Gordon swooped off the branch, followed by Lonnie and Stella. Perkins looked at me and made a quiet cooing sound.

"Yes, you should ride with us in the car," I agreed. Burrowing owls weren't exactly known for flying long distances, or for getting anywhere quickly.

There was a trill, and Stella arced around to settle onto the branch next to Perkins. The toucan looked from Perkins to me, her orange beak whipping back and forth. "You can come in the car, too," I assured her.

Lonnie continued to follow Gordon, her wide, graceful raven's wings easily keeping up with the pelican's pace.

By the time Marlee and I arrived at the tavern, Perkins on my shoulder and Stella flapping alongside Marlee, the other two familiars were already there. Gordon and Lonnie had settled on top of the shelves of liquor and potions behind the bar. Perkins and Stella followed suit while Valerian laughed. "I knew my coven was on its way as soon as these two flew inside. You're not here for a drink, are you?"

"We're on a mission," Marlee said. "A magical mission."

"For Jo." I explained Jo's request, and Valerian glanced around the tavern. "Give me a few minutes to make sure everyone has what they need, and then I can take a quick break. We can head out back and perform a spell in the alley. I've got just the right one in mind for this."

After pouring two fresh beers and putting in a food order for customers, Valerian told us she was ready to go.

"Do we need anything for this spell?" I asked as Marlee and I slid off our stools.

Valerian had already been walking toward the back door, but she stopped and turned on her heel. "Oh, yes. Hang on." She popped behind the bar and reached into a gray earthenware pot with a lid on it. When she extracted her hand, I saw she had not an herb or a crystal, but an entire bundle of something wrapped in a gold cloth. "I keep this on hand for patrons who need a little something extra in the luck department."

"Your Good Mojo Martini isn't enough?" I asked.

"Spread these items out around one of those drinks, and you're going to get an even bigger boost of good fortune," Valerian assured me.

I had unbuttoned my coat once we got inside the tavern, but I hastily closed it up again as soon as I passed through the door and into the alley. Unlike the street out front, which was lined with sidewalks and plenty of trees and other plants, the alley was strictly utilitarian. There was a narrow drive for cars, and bins for garbage and recycling were lined up behind every place of business along that side of Main Street.

Valerian looked around while our familiars, who had followed us out the door, flew around her head with interest. "I don't want to put these items in the middle of the alley, in case someone drives past. Let's clear ourselves a little space closer to the building."

Marlee and I immediately got to work, moving the bins close together so there would be more room for us to perform the spell.

As I rolled the garbage bin out of the way, I spotted something on the ground behind it, wedged into the narrow strip of dirt that separated the asphalt from the edge of the tavern's back wall. It looked like a small bag, or maybe a large purse, and it was made from a quilted green and pink paisley fabric.

"Was someone trying to toss this into the bin, but they missed?" I mused as I reached for the long strap attached to the bag. That theory didn't seem likely. It looked more like the bag had been placed there on purpose.

I lifted it up onto the lid of the garbage bin. Bracing myself for what I might find inside, I slowly unzipped the top while leaning back. Living in a magical town, there was no telling what might come flying out of it.

Nothing flew out, as it happened, and I leaned my face closer to peer into the dark interior of the bag.

It was absolutely stuffed with cash.

Chapter Thirteen

"This is definitely not trash," I said. "Val, Marlee, come look!"

Valerian gasped when she spotted the money, then gave me a self-satisfied look. "We haven't even done the spell for luck, but it's already working. I told you this bundle of items brought good fortune!"

Marlee reached out a tentative hand, her fingers stopping just short of the bag. "Don't touch it anymore, Hazel! We're calling the constables to come get this!"

I snatched my hands away, as if I'd been scalded. "Oh! You think it might be related to Wanda's murder, don't you?"

"Who knows?" Marlee was looking up and down the alley, as if whomever had stashed the money might still be nearby. "This is strange, and Wanda's murder was strange, and I have a hard time believing they're separate incidents. Call it a gut instinct. I think you need to call your boyfriend."

A surprised laugh escaped my lips. "You're teasing me about Wyatt in the middle of this situation?"

Marlee hitched up a shoulder in a little shrug. "It's just money, not a dead body."

I grumbled, for what felt like the hundredth time, about Wyatt not being my boyfriend, but I did call him. He was surprised at my news and promised he and some other constables would be there in less than ten minutes.

One of the things I loved about living in Foxfire Haven again was how one could get anywhere in such a short amount of time.

"If it is related to Wanda's murder," Valerian said as we waited, "then how? She wasn't killed so someone could steal this money from her, or they would have it."

"Maybe it was a hired killer, and we just intercepted the payment." Marlee's eyes were wide. "Maybe this is the drop-off point for the killer's fee."

I nearly laughed out loud at that idea, but someone had put that money there for a reason, and "hired killer" seemed just as likely as any other reason I could think of.

Two sedans that read *Foxfire Haven Constables* on the side turned into the alley in well under ten minutes. By then, our speculating had taken an even wilder turn, and we had even floated the idea that the money was wholly unrelated to the murder, and was actually a ransom payment for a kidnapping we had yet to learn about.

Before long, Wyatt and two other constables were huddled around the bag of money, silently evaluating the situation. They, clearly, weren't jumping to the same absurd conclusions we were.

"You found it here?" Wyatt asked.

"It was behind the trash bin," I said, pointing. "We were moving the bins so we could lay out some items for a spell."

One of the constables began to take photos of the area, and the other put on plastic gloves so he could move the bag without getting any of his own fingerprints or DNA on it.

"Maybe Wanda was going to make Sam a cash offer for the newspaper," I blurted.

"Oh, I like that theory." Valerian held her hands up, palms facing each other but not touching. "We're close to the newspaper office, so maybe Wanda stashed the bag here when she realized someone was coming after her."

"Maybe," Wyatt said, emphasizing the word, "you ladies should leave the speculating to the pros."

I felt a little silly for having come up with such crazy ideas, but Valerian seemed unfazed. "You have to admit, we've got some good theories. I have to get back to work. Marlee, Haze, you two fill me in later."

We promised to do just that, but it was soon apparent that our report was going to be a lackluster one. The bag was put in the back of one of the cars, a few more photos were taken, and that was that.

Wyatt and I still hadn't had a real conversation since our blowup at the breakfast table. I wasn't sure I was ready to discuss that little disagreement, but there was one thing I wanted to talk to him about before he slid back into his car and left. I called his name and waved him over to a spot a short distance away from the other constables.

"Did Uncle Grant ever talk about a ghost at the funeral home?" I asked him in a low voice. Only Marlee could hear us.

"Of course. I always asked about that fussy ghost whenever I ran into Grant. It was interesting to finally meet him yesterday."

"No, I don't mean Holman. This would be another ghost. A man, we think. One who can throw things across the room."

Wyatt had been looking at me warily, probably worried I was going to restart our disagreement about me spying on Jo, but his expression quickly turned concerned. "Throw things? Is this a violent haunting?"

I spread my hands. "I don't know. I hope not. At any rate, nothing has been thrown directly at one of us."

Wyatt shook his head. "Grant never mentioned any activity like that. Then again, he and I weren't close. You should ask one of his good friends what they might know."

There was absolutely no way I was going to pose the question to Grant's former best friend, Roscoe, since he'd turned on Grant in his later years and was determined to treat me with just as much vitriol. I knew Barry had really liked Grant, though, so I would start with him. I thanked Wyatt, and then the constables were gone.

Marlee went inside the tavern, and she returned with Valerian on her heels.

"Let's do this quick!" Valerian said. "I've got a group of tourists who are going to be needing a second round soon."

Valerian wasted no time laying out the items bundled inside the gold fabric, which included tiger's eye, a small carved figure of a turtle, and one vanilla bean inside a glass vial. There was also, I noticed, a silver pendant in the shape of a four-leafed clover.

The spell wasn't nearly as simple as I had expected. Over time, I'd come to realize that many of Valerian's favorite spells were short and easy, but this spell for luck was a bit more complicated. Inside the bundle, there was even a sheet of paper with the incantation written on it, since it was quite long.

When we were finished, Valerian quickly scooped up all the items from the ground, then Marlee and I moved the bins back into place. Maybe, I thought, Valerian really had been right, and we had been lucky to find that money. I hoped the constables would figure out where the mystery money came from soon, because I was curious to know if it did, in fact, have anything to do with Wanda's murder.

The familiars, who had perched on top of a nearby van to watch the spell, began flapping their wings. "Come on," I said to Perkins while Marlee walked over and scooped her toucan into her hands. Gordon and Lonnie both rose into the air, and I knew we would see them back at the house.

The group of tourists Valerian had mentioned were just finishing up their first round of drinks when the three of us—plus Perkins and Stella—came inside. They were already a bit rowdy, and I had no interest in sticking around to see how much louder they might get with every fresh drink. Instead, I texted Jo that we'd just sent some luck her way, and then Marlee and I headed home.

As we pulled into the driveway in Marlee's car, I started to laugh. "Are we stuck in a loop? I've seen this before."

There was a sedan parked in front of the house, and I recognized it as the same rental I'd seen a few days before. Once again, Nicole was standing on the front porch.

"Think she's going to make another offer for the house?" I asked as Marlee pulled to a stop. "Maybe Wanda wants to buy the place from beyond the grave!"

"Let's hope that woman doesn't come back as a ghost" was Marlee's response. "Could you imagine being haunted by both her and Holman? It would be unbearable!"

"Hi, Nicole," I called as I came up the porch steps. "I'm glad you're here. I wanted to check and see how you were doing. Are you holding up okay?"

Nicole had one hand gripped around something small and metallic, but she waved her free hand dismissively. "I'm doing all right. In fact, I'm here for an interview."

Frankly, I would have been less surprised if Nicole *had* made yet another offer on the house. She knew I owned a delivery service, but surely she realized I was a one-woman operation. Still, I felt a wave of sympathy for her. She was in a town where she hardly knew anyone, her boss had just been murdered, and she was very unexpectedly—and very suddenly—unemployed.

"You've already started searching for a new job, then," I said. "I figured you'd head back to Florida and find something there. I appreciate that you want to work for Dead Easy Delivery, but I'm not busy enough to need an employee. I'd be happy to help you set up an interview with someone else, though, if I hear of anyone with an opening."

Nicole laughed. "No, I'm not here for a job interview! This is an interview for a story. I'm writing a piece for the newspaper, and I want to get quotes from people in town who knew Wanda. The story is about her."

Chapter Fourteen

My chest tightened in sudden panic. There was absolutely no way I was going to give a quote about Wanda for the newspaper. I had nothing good to say about her, and I wasn't willing to go on record talking about what a brash bully she had been.

Instead, what I said to Nicole was, "I didn't know you were a writer! I thought you were Wanda's personal assistant."

"I have my degree in journalism," Nicole clarified. It was only then I realized the small object in her hand was a digital tape recorder. "I started as a staff writer for the *Osbourne Observer*, which Wanda bought shortly after I was hired there. She decided she wanted me to work directly for her."

Nicole was saying it like Wanda had bestowed an honor on her, but I very much doubted that was the case. People like Jo, who absolutely adored being a writer and telling stories that mattered, wouldn't find much fulfillment doing something like making travel arrangements—or throwing out wild offers on a house that wasn't even for sale—for someone else.

"How long were you her PA?" Marlee asked.

"Five years." Nicole rolled her shoulders back and stood a little taller. "My magical specialty is logistics and organization. Wanda said she couldn't do without me. She even told me I wasn't allowed to date, because a relationship would take too much of my time."

Maybe my original theory had been right: after years of loyal service to a selfish, demanding woman, Nicole had snapped and killed her boss.

She could have simply quit her job instead of resorting to murder, I reminded myself.

Since I wasn't willing to outright ask Nicole if she had killed Wanda, I said, "My magic is of a similar nature. I joke that I'm a spreadsheet witch."

"We're the witches who have our acts together." Nicole smiled, then raised the tape recorder. "I'd just like to get a brief quote about your relationship with Wanda."

Being cornered by the woman hardly counted as a relationship. "I only briefly met her," I said. "I'm afraid I can't give you a good quote."

Well, at least it was an honest response.

"I understand she talked to you herself about buying this place." The tape recorder was even closer to me now, a red light on it blinking ominously.

"Yeah," I said slowly. Suddenly, I wasn't thinking of quotes or newspaper articles. I was thinking about that bag of money. If it had belonged to Wanda, maybe she had been planning to make a cash offer for the funeral home. It was possible Wanda had thought I would cave to her request if I was staring into the depths of a bag full of money.

"Did she give you a figure?" Nicole prompted.

I blinked and returned my attention to the woman in front of me. "Oh, no. We didn't get that far. Like I said, we only met briefly. I really can't comment on her, since she and I barely spoke to each other."

Nicole's shoulders drooped a bit, but she kept her professionalism. "I understand. I'll try some other people I know she met. Thanks, anyway."

As Nicole was walking down the porch steps, I finally remembered my manners. "My condolences, Nicole."

"Thanks," she called airily, not even turning back toward me.

"Well, that was interesting," Marlee commented as we watched Nicole drive away. Her voice was laden with sarcasm as she continued, "I'm disappointed she didn't ask me for a quote. I would have enjoyed giving her my honest opinion about Wanda."

"Surely she didn't think I would have anything positive to say."

"Maybe that was the point."

I gave Marlee a curious glance. "I assumed she was writing some sweet tribute to her beloved boss. You think it's more of an exposé?"

"I guess we'll have to wait until it's published to find out. In the meantime, I'll be in the dining room if you need anything. I have a mountain of tasks to get through for this memorial party."

Unlike Marlee, I did not have a lot of work to do, but I was feeling restless. I wound up in the garage, where I was determined to take inventory of the odd assortment of things stacked all around the hearse. I had given the task a half-hearted start about a month before, then quickly given up. There must have been half a century's worth of junk piled in that garage, and going through all of it was a bit of an intimidating task.

Perkins, at least, was willing to help out. He came along as I went into the garage, rolled up the sleeves of my sweater, and started pulling objects out of an old wooden crate. I found brake pads—probably off the hearse—old street maps, and a few stray tools.

There was also yet another photograph that I attributed to Grant. The shot was of one of the former chapel rooms—meaning it was either Marlee's or Valerian's room—all decorated for a funeral service. There was no casket in the arched recess between the stained-glass windows, but there were enormous flower arrangements and wooden columns with thick white pillar candles burning brightly atop them.

The edges of the photo were dog-eared, and there was a scratch down one side of it. It was no wonder, since it had been tossed into a crate full of tools and car parts. Nevertheless, I took the photo to the workbench so I could look at it under the work light there. I held the photo close to my face and scanned it slowly, but there was no sign of anyone in it, living or dead.

Perkins fluttered onto the workbench and gazed up at me. Then, he hopped closer, bent low, and tapped his beak against the backside of the photo. I flipped it over, thinking there might be writing there, but there wasn't.

There was, however, a date printed on the back. The photo had been taken the same year I graduated high school. "It's ancient," I joked.

Perkins bounced his head up and down several times. I had once thought it was his way of agreeing with me, but by the time I was in my mid-twenties, I had realized it was his way of telling me I had missed the point. *Go on, try again* was my best interpretation of the head-bob.

I turned the photo over again and re-examined the backside, but still, all I saw was the date it had been printed. "Oh! That's the point, isn't it, Perky? I keep finding all these photos Grant took, and maybe, we need to put them in chronological order. We can look at the photo with the bearded ghost in it to find out when it was taken, too."

And, I suspected, the date of that photo and when Grant had started acting erratically would be from around the same time. I didn't have proof his behavior was related to the paranormal activity in the house, but it seemed like a strong possibility.

I had moved on to sorting through the junk in a crumbling cardboard box—and it was truly junk, including torn paper Christmas decorations and a few cancelled checks from the nineteen fifties—when Marlee joined me.

"You look like you're having a ball," she said, "but would you be willing to take a break to make a couple of delivery runs for the party?"

I instantly dropped the stained linen lampshade I had picked up. "Yes, please. What do you need?"

"I need you to go get some big urns—"

"Like for someone who's been cremated?"

Marlee screwed up her face. "Ew, no! I mean the big silver ones for serving coffee at events. The tea shop has a few we're going to borrow, and I'm buying their coffee blend. It's every bit as good as the tea there. Then, I need you to head to the library. Even though Wanda didn't buy the newspaper, Sam still wants it to be well-represented at this party, so the library is loaning us a few framed pages of it from their archives."

I gave Marlee a little salute, and Perkins cooed enthusiastically. We would both be happy to get out of the garage. "Sounds easy enough. I'll see you in a couple hours."

Back to Realitea hadn't opened until after I'd moved out of Foxfire Haven at eighteen. Even though I didn't have any fond childhood memories associated with it, the cozy place had quickly become one of my favorite spots in town. There was lace absolutely everywhere, and the mint-green color scheme always made me think of the walls of my old elementary school, but there was something sweet and homey about the place. It even had a resident cat, who was also adorned in lace and mint green. The elegant collar gave the black-and-white cat a sophisticated air.

The owner of the shop, Millie, was exactly what I expected of a place like Back to Realitea. She had short black hair that curled a bit wildly and was shot with streaks of white, her white apron was edged with ruffles of lace, and she had full cheeks that seemed to be perpetually red, like she'd just been outside in the cold.

Millie also had just a trace of a British accent, and when I asked where she was from, she told me she'd moved to Foxfire Haven from Knightspell. The small seaside town in England was one of the top destinations for magical tourism, and it was somewhere I hoped to visit someday.

At Millie's direction, I pulled up to the back door of the tea shop and wheeled the gurney into the kitchen. Between the two of us, we quickly loaded the urns—for coffee not bodies—onto the gurney, as well as a box containing bags of both regular and decaf coffee.

"It's ironic I'm getting paid for something dedicated to that woman," Millie said. She looked so cheery, but I could hear the bite in her voice. "She came in here acting like she was queen of the magical world, and after insisting I give her a free scone so she could, and I quote, 'start getting to know her new local tea shop,' she began to throw out pricing for newspaper ads."

"I did hear she had a rather aggressive approach, and a big plan to make money by selling more ads than Sam currently does."

"She was downright mean. She told me that I would need to buy an ad that was not smaller than half a page and ran every Sunday for at least three months if I wanted her to write a sweet editorial about my tea shop. As if I can afford that kind of thing! This is Foxfire Haven, not New York City."

"I got the impression Wanda was pretty wealthy," I said. "She wanted to buy my home, in fact. I wonder if she used the same approach with the newspaper she bought down in Florida, exchanging expensive ads for glowing editorials."

"She hinted that if I didn't buy the ad, there would be an article about the shop, anyway, but it would definitely not be a positive one."

I wasn't really surprised by that tidbit, since it sounded right in line with the things I already knew about Wanda, but that didn't make it any less scandalous in my book. "That's extortion," I grumbled as I heaved an urn into the back of the hearse.

And, if Wanda was making those kinds of veiled threats, had a business owner in town decided to stop her before she could take everyone's money or ruin a place that couldn't afford her exorbitant fees?

The suspect list might be much, much longer than I thought.

"Anyway," Millie continued, "I suppose someone was going to take Wanda up on the advertising deal, since the police found that bag of cash."

Slowly, I straightened up and turned to face Millie as the urn slid away from me on the rollers built into the hearse. "You think that money might have been from a local business owner?"

"I do. I heard a rumor that the day Wanda died, she told the clerk at her hotel that she was off to meet someone who wanted to make a deal with her."

Chapter Fifteen

WELL. THAT WAS CERTAINLY a new twist. If, that was, the gossip at all resembled the truth.

"Maybe Wanda was going to make a deal with someone, but that doesn't mean it was a potential advertiser for the newspaper," I pointed out. "She hadn't even purchased the paper yet."

"I heard the bag had the logo for a local shop on it," Millie continued. "Unfortunately, by the time the rumor reached me, the shop name wasn't a part of the tale."

I shut my eyes briefly and pulled up the memory of the scene in the alley. The bag had been made of a quilted material, but had there been a logo printed on it somewhere? And if so, how had I missed it? Of course, as busy as the paisley print was, my own name could have been on that bag, and I probably wouldn't have noticed. I had also been a little distracted by what was inside the bag.

If I run into Wyatt, I'll ask him. Or maybe Val and Marlee caught a detail I didn't.

I thanked Millie for her help loading up, and I was delighted when she sent me home with a sample of a new tea blend she was trying out. I promised to give her feedback on it the next time I visited Back to Realitea.

That night, we were one exhausted coven. Jo was trying to do her job while juggling all the curious visitors, gossip, and the ongoing stress of having no idea who had killed Wanda, or why. Marlee had gotten a lot of work done in preparation for Wanda's memorial party, but she was so tired she kept trying to scoop up her potato salad at dinner with a knife instead of a fork.

Valerian was worn out, too, but she had a smile on her face. "Murder is really good for business, and tips," she had told us happily. As the gathering spot for local gossip, the tavern had been busier than usual the last few days. "Although, I did catch a few folks poking around in odd places. I think some people showed up just to see if there's more money stashed somewhere."

As we were cleaning up from dinner, Jo said, "I know we're all really tired—"

"But," the rest of us chimed in.

"But, I think we should do a quick Rest and Reset spell. Sure, it will sap even more energy, but it will help us all get a good night's sleep, and then we can wake up and tackle tomorrow with fresh minds."

"Tomorrow is my last full day for party prep," Marlee said. "I could definitely use some magical help."

"And I'll be doing a couple of regular deliveries, plus more for Marlee," I said. "A fresh mind is exactly what I need."

Valerian pulled a crumpled five-dollar bill out of the pocket of her black jeans. "And I'll be raking in more tips tomorrow night. A Friday night, and a murder, and a mysterious bag of cash? Oh, yeah, the tavern will be packed. I need some good rest before making all those drinks!"

"After we do the spell," I added, "I'll brew a pot of tea as a reward for ourselves. It's a new blend Millie at the tea shop asked me to taste-test."

Jo quickly gave us a rundown of what the spell would entail, and then we split up to grab various items for it. I was responsible for gathering something that represented rest, so I grabbed one of the pillows off my bed. I also got a handful of dried chamomile to add to the cauldron.

Starlight was one of the things that could aid the spell, according to Jo, so she suggested we bundle up and head to our usual spot in the backyard. Our familiars followed us outside, taking up their favorite perch on the edge of the garage roof. Perkins was wedged between Gordon and Stella, so I knew he was feeling nice and toasty, despite the cold temperature.

We had a small folding table we used for outdoor spell casting, so we quickly set it up and covered it with a green scarf Marlee had retrieved from her closet.

Jo added the chamomile to the cauldron, along with lavender and bergamot, plus a pinch of vervain. Marlee lit a black candle, then carefully touched the flame to the mixture inside the cauldron as Jo started reciting the incantation. The mixed herbs gave off an earthy, relaxing scent as they began to smoke.

"Val, go ahead and place the crystals you brought around the cauldron," Jo instructed. "Put the moonstone facing east, since the moon rises from that direction."

Valerian did as instructed, and Jo returned to the incantation. Her voice was soothing, and even though the breeze was bitingly cold against my face, I felt my body starting to loosen up. I turned my eyes upward, soaking in the view of the stars overhead. There were just a few long, feathery clouds stretching across the sky, so we had a mostly clear view. A waning moon hovered above the line of Douglas firs that stood along the back edge of the property.

"Now," Jo said, "everyone close your eyes, and imagine drifting off into a peaceful sleep."

That was an easy instruction to follow.

"Picture yourself dreaming of something sweet while you have a small smile on your lips."

My mind raced through a few potential sweet-dream scenarios, but none of them felt quite right. I imagined identifying Wanda's killer, taking a walk along a sunny beach in a warm tropical location, and spending a lovely spring afternoon planting flowers in the front yard.

I even pictured having coffee with Wyatt and us getting along the entire time.

Finally, my imagination landed on an image of me teaching Hailey a control spell. That felt right. I sensed the joy of teaching my granddaughter magic, the satisfied smile on her face, and the way she would wave her arms in excited triumph when she was successful.

I was so absorbed in the mental image it took me a moment to realize Jo was talking to me. "Hazel. Haze! Put the pillow on the table."

I opened my eyes and did as instructed, and Jo balanced a small silver dagger on top of it. "We cut through the stress and the noise to find sweet rest," she chanted.

My mind shifted back to the idea of finding Wanda's killer. Then, I imagined what the scene must have looked like when she died.

I gave myself a shake. That was not the kind of mental image that would bring me sweet dreams. Unfortunately, though, the harder I tried to return to pleasant thoughts, the more bad things I imagined.

I saw Wyatt again, but this time, he was standing up angrily, shoving his teacup away from him.

Stop, stop, stop! I yelled silently.

But it was too late. My magic spiked, and there was no way I could hold all of it inside. I opened my eyes again. "Watch out!" I shouted, right as a wave of pink magic burst out of my body. Valerian quickly stepped one foot backward, giving her a wider stance to withstand the onslaught. Marlee ducked, and Jo snatched up the pillow, holding it in front of herself like a shield.

The table wobbled, rose up onto two legs, then settled back down. The cauldron on top of it tipped over, spilling some of the still-smoking herbs onto Marlee's scarf.

I leaped forward and snatched the scarf off the table. Unfortunately, I wasn't like those magicians who could remove a tablecloth without disturbing the dishes atop it. The cauldron rolled right off the edge of the table and landed upside-down in the dead grass while the herbs went flying.

Marlee jumped up and began to stamp on the smoldering herbs with her feet. The last thing we needed was to start a fire.

I heard a strange noise and looked over to see Jo with her face buried in the pillow.

"Oh, no. Did I hurt you, Jo?"

Jo lowered the pillow. Her eyes were scrunched closed, and her shoulders were shaking. At first, I thought she was crying, but then she let out a guffaw. "I'm sorry," Jo said. She was laughing so hard she could barely speak, and she actually snorted. "It's just, here we are, trying to relax, and *bam*!" She hugged the pillow against her body.

Marlee began to giggle, followed by Valerian.

My embarrassment about the uncontrolled magic began to diminish. It really was a ridiculous situation, and I gave in and laughed along with my coven. "Sorry, ladies," I said. "I really hope the spell will still work."

"Honestly," Marlee said, wiping at one eye, "I think it made the spell better. I've been so stressed about this last-minute event, and laughing just feels good."

"Yeah," Jo said. "That's the first time I've laughed since Wanda showed up in Foxfire Haven. I feel physically lighter now. Thank you, Hazel."

"Um, you're welcome?" I held up Marlee's scarf. "If I singed this, I'll buy you a new one, Marlee."

But Marlee waved a hand. "It's got a chocolate stain on one corner, plus a couple of snags from a run-in I had with a thorny plant. Scorch marks will fit right in."

I was so grateful to have friends like these, and I said so as we began to clean up the chaos my magical exhalation had caused. Everyone agreed it had been unexpected but surprisingly fitting, and when I went to bed, Jo told me she hoped my dreams were the opposite of whatever had made my magic build up so quickly.

Thankfully, I woke up the next morning with no memory at all of my dreams.

When I walked into the kitchen and saw Jo, though, I had to wonder if the spell hadn't worked for her. She had a small stack of papers in front of her, and I recognized her handwriting on the topmost sheet. Another piece of paper was in her hands, and she was slowly tearing it to shreds. Already, there was a pile of torn paper on the table, and Gordon was dutifully guarding it.

"Jo." I managed to turn it into a question, and I was so concerned for her I sat right down at the table rather than getting my usual cup of coffee first.

"If I don't have any intentions sitting around, then they can't be used against me."

Something stirred in my memory as I watched small shreds of paper float down onto the table. I couldn't quite place what it reminded me of, though. "What do you mean?"

Jo heaved a sigh. "I mean I'm destroying every intention I ever wrote. The constables noticed one I'd pinned to my office wall, and they want me to come in for questioning because the intention made them think I might have killed Wanda Whitcomb."

CHAPTER SIXTEEN

I WAS SO SHOCKED I couldn't speak immediately. When I did finally open my mouth, what came out was a lot of stuttering and incredulous noises.

"Exactly," Jo said in a flat tone. She picked up another sheet of paper and began tearing it up.

"The constables think you killed Wanda with your manifesting magic?" I finally said.

Jo shook her head. "No, they think I killed her by stabbing her in the neck with a fountain pen. But the intention was worded in such a way that they think I had motive."

"Did the constables specifically say that?" I asked. Out of the corner of my eye, I saw Valerian come into the kitchen from the hallway, and she leaned against the doorframe, her arms across her chest as she listened to our conversation.

"The woman who called me from the station said they had noticed an intention on the wall of my office, and they had some follow-up questions about it." Jo opened her hand, palm down, and tiny bits of paper fluttered to the table.

“What did the intention say?” I just couldn’t imagine what Jo could have written that the constables might have interpreted as malicious.

“It was about me breaking through obstacles in my career so I could achieve my desired success.” Jo started shredding again.

“Oh, they can’t really think something that generic means you killed someone,” Valerian said. “When are they coming here to talk to you?”

“I have to go to them, at nine o’clock. I plan to have all these shredded and burned before I leave.”

“Do you want me to go with you to the station?” Valerian asked.

“I’ll come with you, too, Jo,” I said.

“We’ll all go!” Marlee squeezed into the doorway next to Valerian. “Why are we going to the constable station, anyway? I just heard Val offer to go.”

Jo explained her situation, and when she was done, Marlee said, “But you came home after work the night Wanda was killed, and Hazel and I were here with you. We’re your alibis.”

“But I didn’t get home until half an hour after leaving the office, because I was driving around trying to get my anger under control.”

Marlee made a noise of impatience. “The constables really don’t have much to go on, do they? But, we’ll do everything we can to help you.” She clapped her hands together, like she was calling us to order. “Hazel, you help Jo tear up those papers. Val, please pour coffee for all of us. I’m going to make us a quick breakfast. We’re going to need our strength to deal with this.”

I couldn't help but smile at Marlee as I reached for one of Jo's intentions. She had gone right into event-planning mode to make sure Jo's trip to the station went as smoothly as it could.

Sometimes, I thought, *you don't need magic. You just need teamwork and tight planning.*

Holman materialized next to Valerian as she was placing coffee cups in front of Jo and me. "You should wear a nice dress," he told Jo. "That yellow one you have looks beautiful with your skin tone. You should wear that."

Jo's lips thinned into a tight line. "I might be a suspect in a murder case, and you want to give me fashion advice?"

"It's exactly why I'm suggesting that dress!" Holman looked affronted. "A well-dressed person is less likely to get arrested."

"That is not true," Valerian said.

"It most certainly is."

"Prove it."

"Thank you, Holman," I said, raising my voice to stop the brewing argument. "We appreciate your concern for Jo, and she will take your suggestion under consideration."

Jo opened her mouth, looking like she was about to protest, then gave Holman an impatient smile. "Yes, I'll think about it. Goodbye, Holman."

"Why do I even bother?" the ghost mumbled as he disappeared.

By eight forty-five, Jo's intentions were nothing but ashes in the grill on the back porch, and we were all full of pancakes and coffee. It was time to head to the Foxfire Haven constable station.

Jo elected to wear a plum-colored blouse with pinstriped charcoal pants. Holman, thankfully, didn't show up to argue the point.

Marlee drove us all to the station, and as we walked slowly toward the front door, Jo said wistfully, "I am so tired of being part of the news. I just want to write about it."

"So does she," I said, pointing. Nicole was hovering near the front door, her digital tape recorder in one hand and a small notebook in the other.

Nicole's eyes darted from one of us to the other. "Hazel, why is your entire coven here?" she asked. Her tone was clipped and businesslike, a reporter speaking to a person involved in a news story. The bit of warmth she'd had in our earlier encounters was gone entirely.

Valerian answered before I could, and she was much more direct than I would have been. "That is our business, not yours."

Inside, there was a wide desk with a constable sitting behind it. Chairs occupied the rest of the room for people waiting to speak with one of the constables. Only a few people were waiting when we walked inside, but I did spot Wyatt standing in the doorway that led to the rest of the station.

He rubbed the palms of both hands along his cheeks, which were covered in black-and-silver stubble. "Of course all of you came." He sounded like the most long-suffering man in the world.

"We're here to support Jo," I told him.

"You're all going to have to wait here for her," Wyatt countered. "She's not allowed to have friends along for the ride."

"But I'll know they're out here, and that's enough," Jo said. "I'm not really alone, even if they can't go into this with me."

"You could have a lawyer, though," Valerian pointed out.

"No. I've got this." Jo squared her shoulders and let Wyatt lead her down the hallway. The rest of us watched until she'd turned through a doorway and was out of sight.

Marlee whimpered quietly, like she was in pain. "There are so many strong emotions here," she complained. "Anxiety, fear, pressure, and something else. It's like frustration, but stronger. Exasperation, maybe."

"That last one would be from Wyatt, I'm sure," I said.

We all sat down, with Marlee between Valerian and me. We each took one of Marlee's hands in an attempt to bolster her against all the emotions she was soaking up. In exchange, the connection helped me, as well, and I felt a sense of calm settling over me as we waited.

Just twenty minutes later, Jo walked into the reception area, looking grim but not upset.

Plus, she wasn't in handcuffs, so that was a good sign.

The three of us quickly rose and gathered around her. "Well?" Valerian prompted.

"I didn't need that yellow dress, after all," Jo said in answer.

Wyatt was right behind Jo, and since she seemed okay, I jumped at my chance to ask him, "Is it true that bag we found in the alley had a label for a local business on it?"

"What sort of things have you been hearing?" Wyatt asked. His eyes glinted.

There was a laugh from the constable sitting behind the desk. "Nikki Naito was way too classy for labels!"

Wyatt threw an angry glance at the constable. When he turned back to me, I involuntarily took a step back. There was a look in his eyes that told me he was at the end of his rope. "I blame you, Hazel."

I knew I had done plenty of things to annoy Wyatt in the past, but in this instance, I couldn't figure out what I could have done. "What are you blaming me for?"

"For my team not keeping their mouths shut."

"Ah, so the bag is from this Nikki brand, then."

Wyatt made a growling sound in his throat.

Undaunted, I added, "Is she a suspect?"

Valerian chuckled. "I should have recognized that bag as her work."

"And I don't own a Nikki Naito," Jo said, "so not only did I not kill Wanda, but that bag of money wasn't mine, either."

"But this is a good lead, right?" I asked, giving Wyatt what I hoped was an encouraging look. "You can get a list of her customers. Maybe she remembers who she sold that bag to!"

"Wow, why didn't we think of that?" The sarcasm was so thick I took another step back. "It seems simple, but Nikki died two years ago and left no sales records. It's a dead end."

Chapter Seventeen

A SNORT ESCAPED MY nose while I pinched my lips together as tightly as I could to stop myself from laughing. Marlee and Valerian both snickered, and when I looked at Jo, she was pressing two fingers against her lips and looking anywhere but at Wyatt.

"Dead end?" Valerian's shoulders shook with silent laughter.

"Did you say that on purpose?" I asked Wyatt.

"The four of you are going to be the death of me," Wyatt muttered.

"Oh, are you investigating us for your own murder, too?" Valerian asked.

Jo turned away, still desperately trying not to laugh.

Wyatt pointed at me. "I had a nice, normal life until you moved back to Foxfire Haven."

"What have I done?" *Other than yell at you about your cat going after Perkins, bother you at all hours, dive headfirst into your murder investigations, and annoy you so much you don't even drink the tea I make you.*

Oh. I really had disrupted Wyatt's life.

Maybe Wyatt was too exasperated to respond to my question, or maybe, he could see I'd already worked out the answer for myself. Either way, he turned away and stalked down the hallway, in the direction of his office. He was muttering as he went, and I thought I heard him say something about our coven and "all her fault."

"Come on," I said to the others. "Let's get Jo out of here."

"I have a bit of time before I have to be at the tavern," Valerian said. "How about some tea?"

We all quickly agreed to that, and since Back to Realitea was on a side street near city hall, it was a short drive to get there. Soon, we were seated in plush chairs around a table topped by a mint-green tablecloth and a lace doily.

"It really wasn't bad," Jo said when we asked her how harrowing her experience had been. "Wyatt was very polite."

I started to say something snarky in response to that, but I stopped myself. Wyatt and I didn't get along all that often, but whenever I'd seen him in action as chief constable, he'd been every bit the professional. Of course he had treated Jo respectfully.

"Did you tell him that it was dumb of anyone to think your intention implied murder?" Valerian asked.

Jo made a motion with her head that was half nod, half shake. "I didn't put it quite like that, but I told him that I'd only ever written positive intentions, and that it should have been clear from the one on the wall of my office that I had never intended harm to anyone. Besides, I wrote that ages before I even knew Wanda existed. It's dated two years ago!"

"I hope you pointed that out, too," Marlee said.

"I did. Wyatt suggested I could have gotten frustrated that my intention hadn't manifested yet, so I had taken matters into my own hands."

All of us made noises of protest, and people at the other tables looked at us over their teacups with stern expressions.

"However," Jo said before any of us could speak, "Wyatt didn't really believe that. I could tell he was just trying to look at every possibility, even though that one was highly unlikely."

"You could say it was another dead end," I quipped.

Valerian shook her head sadly. "It's a shame Wyatt doesn't see the humor in his accidental puns. He's always so dead serious."

This time, it was our raucous laughter that drew looks from other patrons.

We ordered our tea, as well as scones that were served with strawberry jam and clotted cream, then settled in to discuss the murder in a more clear-minded way.

"This thing about the bag being made by a local," I began, "should still be helpful to the constables, even if the maker died."

"What I wouldn't give for a Nikki Naito," Marlee said, her voice dreamy. "But they're so expensive."

"If they're expensive, then there can't be a lot of them." I was picturing witches clamoring for limited-edition quilted bags. "If it was a local who stuffed that bag with cash, then maybe it won't be that hard to track them down."

Jo pulled out her phone and began typing while Valerian said, "Nikki made those bags for years. It might be harder than you think."

"There are currently six of her bags for sale on Alchemy," Jo announced.

"Alchemy?" I asked, feeling confused.

"You know, the site for buying and selling secondhand items." Marlee paused, then gave a self-conscious laugh. "Online shopping wasn't a thing when you left the magical world. Alchemy is a site for us, and you can buy everything from vintage clothing for dwarves to secondhand spell books."

"Yeah," Jo said, "their tagline is *Transmute Your Garbage Into Gold*."

I laughed at the idea of browsing the internet for used magical items, but it made sense. It was an easy way to connect all the small supernatural towns throughout the country or, even, the world.

"If people are selling their old Nikki Naito bags on Alchemy," Valerian said, "then the owner of the cash could be from anywhere."

"Including Florida." Jo put her phone back into her purse. "By the way, I can't believe Sam is allowing Nicole to do freelance stories for the paper."

"It's a smart move on Sam's part," I pointed out. "I bet locals will all want to read what the woman who knew Wanda best has to say. That means he'll sell some extra copies of any issue Nicole has a story in."

Jo just sighed heavily in answer.

The arrival of the scones got us to finally move away from the topic of Wanda's murder, and by the time Valerian said she had to skedaddle—yes, she actually used that word—we were busy discussing the weather forecast, which was teasing snow for Sunday evening.

"As long as it doesn't snow Saturday night," Marlee said. "I don't want to put on a party if half the town is staying home."

It rarely snowed in Foxfire Haven. Even though it was my first winter since moving back to my hometown, I remembered the chaos even a light snow could cause. People would stay home, declaring the roads too dangerous to drive on, even if only a quarter of an inch of snow fell.

It had always meant a snow day for us school kids, so I had grown up loving the locals' avoidance of driving in winter weather.

Valerian was going to make the short walk to the tavern, and before she left, Marlee reminded her that we had our third magical plant class that night. "I'll be stressed about the party, but there's no way I'm missing it," Marlee promised us.

It was only eleven o'clock by the time we got back to the house, but I had a busy day ahead, so there wasn't a lot of time to dawdle. I fed Perkins, threw in a load of laundry, then pulled out the calendar where I kept a list of my deliveries. Marlee often told me I should go digital, but I liked having a paper planner that didn't require recharging.

I had four deliveries to make that afternoon. Two of them were for Marlee, since we were down to the final day before the memorial party for Wanda. The first delivery on my schedule was for the tavern, so I'd be seeing Valerian again before too long.

First, though, I had to make the drive to the liquor distributor in Stanton. The thirty-minute drive there was exactly what I needed to clear my head. It was one of those winter days where the sky overhead was a solid gray cloud, but on the ground, it felt like I could see every detail of every tree I drove past. There was a clearness in the cold air that just didn't exist during summertime. The view seemed to clear my mind, as well, and by the time I pulled the hearse into one of the loading bays at the distributor, I was singing along with a rock song on the radio and feeling good.

Twenty minutes later, I was on my way back to Foxfire Haven with a hearse-load of crates containing beer, whiskey, and a habanero-infused vodka that would be a great addition to Valerian's Cold Hands, Warm Heart potion.

The tavern's owner met me out back, in the alley, and between the two of us, we had the hearse unloaded in less than five minutes.

That gurney really had been a good idea.

Once that was done, I had a bit of time before I needed to head to the party supply company to pick up the first load of goods for the memorial on Saturday night. So, I headed through the kitchen and came out behind the bar.

Valerian had just turned around, an empty glass in her hand, and she did a double-take. "It's so weird to see you on this side of things that I almost didn't recognize you! Are you considering a new career?"

"Nah, just dropping in to say hi. And to maybe have a Cold Hands, Warm Heart potion."

"Coming right up."

As she got to work, I made my way around the end of the bar. Barry was at his usual perch on one end, and he waved me over with a long arm, then patted the stool beside him.

This is new.

I hopped up onto the stool next to Barry, and he gave me a worried look. "I heard that Jos—er, Jo, got hauled to the constable station," he said.

"She wasn't hauled there, but they did ask her to come in to answer some questions."

"They can't possibly think she killed that woman."

"Even Jo says she doesn't think that's the case. Wyatt and his constables are following every possible lead, but they know Jo's not the murdery type. We all went along with her, and it went pretty smoothly."

Barry's face relaxed, and one side of his mouth turned up in a smile. "It's quite the bond the four of you have as a coven. Mess with one of you, mess with all of you."

I put my hands on my hips. "That's right!" Then, I rested my elbows on the bar and leaned toward Barry so I could talk in a lower voice. "I wanted to ask you something. You and my uncle Grant were friends."

"We were."

"There's a ghost at the funeral home, a former director there."

Barry rolled his eyes. "Holman. Don't get me started. I stopped going inside the funeral home, because every time I did, Holman would show up and start telling me I should accessorize." Barry swept a hand down his arm, ruffling his fur. "What am I supposed to do? Clip a bow on top of my head in a coordinating color?"

I laughed at the mental image. "Holman has some very firm opinions about my fashion choices, as well. But, recently, it's come to our attention that there's another entity at that house. I watched a cigar box whiz across the office, a stack of Marlee's clothes went flying, and our front door opens all by itself. Did Grant ever mention that kind of activity?"

Barry's eyes lit up. "Grant did mention having some paranormal problems once. He actually described it as poltergeist activity, and it sounds similar to what you and your coven are experiencing."

"Did Grant give any specifics?"

Barry looked thoughtful as he gazed at a spot behind the bar. "I remember Grant saying something about the basement, and how a stack of storage boxes wound up scattered all over the floor. There was also mention of equipment in the embalming room. Grant said he would put things neatly away every day, but sometimes, he'd walk into the room in the morning and find stuff laying around. He said it was like someone had been there doing work."

I felt a shiver run up my spine.

"Grant told me he did a spell to lower the energy of the place, and it seemed to work," Barry continued. "With less unattached energy in the atmosphere, it was harder for the poltergeist to do anything, so the activity ceased."

"Grant essentially drained the funeral home's battery, so the ghost couldn't use the energy to haunt the place," I said, nodding. "Holman must have hated the lack of energy. He probably had a harder time materializing." But, I reminded myself, Grant had banished Holman altogether for a full decade. He might not have been present during the battle with the poltergeist. And, by the time Holman had reappeared, Grant was already dead.

Barry was giving me a sly look, his eyes sparkling like he thought something was funny.

"What?"

"You're so good at solving murders, but you haven't figured out your ghost situation. It's so obvious what's happening."

"It is?"

Barry grinned. "Of course. An entire coven of witches is living there now. Talk about raising the energy! That funeral home has probably never been so alive. The poltergeist activity is only going to escalate until you do something about it."

Chapter Eighteen

Barry's words echoed in my head, and I shut my eyes as the room seemed to spin a bit. I felt his hand against my back, supporting me.

"Hazel?"

I opened my eyes to see Barry looking at me with concern. "How long ago did Grant say he'd done that spell to bring down the energy in the funeral home?" My voice was barely above a whisper.

"Oh, I'm not sure. This was years ago. Long before... Back when we were still friends."

In other words, back before Grant had started shutting out the people dearest to him. I suddenly wondered what would have happened if my parents hadn't moved out of Foxfire Haven. Would they have noticed Grant's changing behavior? Would they have been able to intervene before he got obsessed with some alleged treasure hidden inside the funeral home? His one-time best friend, Roscoe, had said Grant was almost single-minded about it in his final years.

Or, I wondered, what would have happened if I'd never moved away? Maybe I could have helped my uncle.

"Energy can be abated, but only temporarily," I said. "What if the ghost has come back? What if the paranormal activity had something to do with Grant becoming so odd?"

Barry slid his hand off my back, only to put it gently on top of my own. "Hazel, your uncle wasn't afraid of ghosts. I don't know what happened to him—none of us do—but I know the way he changed wasn't because of some poltergeist activity. It would take a lot more than his embalming equipment being moved by unseen forces to affect him."

I took a deep breath and closed my eyes briefly. "You're right, Barry. I guess some part of me is scared I'll experience the same thing Grant did. None of us in his family knew he'd changed so drastically. My dad—Grant's brother—died, and Grant seemed normal at the funeral. We heard from him less in the years after that, but none of us were surprised. His bond was with my dad more than the rest of us. We exchanged Christmas cards, and I'd always mail him a birthday card. So, when you started talking about poltergeist activity, my mind started making connections that probably don't exist."

"You have something Grant never did, which is a coven. Those women aren't going to let anything happen to you. Plus, now, the four of you know that a spell to curb excess energy can help stop this activity before it escalates more."

I laughed sardonically. "Except I struggle with building up too much magic. I can just imagine it now: I'll let out a big magical fart, and the entity will use all that energy to rip open every cabinet door in the kitchen!"

Barry made a deep, rumbling sound. "Magical fart? Is that what you call those puffs of excess magic?"

I didn't usually call it that in front of anyone but my coven, and I nodded my head, feeling silly.

"I like it." Barry laughed again, then his expression turned sad. "I've always regretted not trying to intervene with Grant. He kept pushing me away when I'd try to talk to him, and I realize now I gave up too easily. So, I'm going to promise you, Hazel Underwood, that if you ever start acting like he did, I'm going to make sure we get you the answers you need to overcome it."

I was surprised to feel tears forming, and I blinked quickly. Barry and I didn't know each other well, and this unexpected offer of support reminded me how grateful I was to be back in Foxfire Haven and to have such kind people in my life. "Thanks," I said quietly as I leaned sideways and wrapped my arms around his chest in a hug.

Barry seemed startled by the gesture, and he tensed for a moment before he relaxed, and his arms encircled my shoulders. He smelled like fir trees and line-dried laundry.

There was a quiet *thunk* in front of me, and I let go of Barry to see Valerian standing there with the potion I'd ordered.

"You'd better fill her in," Barry said, nodding his head in Valerian's direction. He drained his whiskey glass, then clapped me on the shoulder. "Keep me posted, Hazel."

"Thank you, Barry. Have a good afternoon."

The second Barry was out of earshot, Valerian leaned over the bar and rested her chin in her hands. "Well. It seems Wyatt has some competition."

I had just taken a sip of the potion, and I thought for sure it was going to fly out of my nose as I started to laugh. Once I'd managed to swallow, I shook my head. "Barry and I are just getting to be friends. I think he feels bad about not being there for Grant, and he's determined to make it right with another member of the family. Besides, he's hinted that there's a broken heart under all that fur."

"He doesn't need to hint. It's kind of obvious, considering he's here almost every day to sulk. Besides, Marlee can feel it when she's in the same place as him." Valerian was still peering at me. "Anyway, I could tell you two weren't flirting with each other. I was just teasing about that. But you were discussing something serious."

"We were. Barry confirmed that we likely have a second ghost in the funeral home, and he suggested that the energy our coven raises by living there is giving that ghost a charge."

"That explains why I saw my toothbrush fly off the sink last week."

"Barry said Grant described it as poltergeist activity, and Marlee and I have also experienced things that fall right in line with that."

Valerian rocked back and planted her hands on the bar. "Right, then. What are we going to do about this ghost? We need to have a coven brainstorming session tonight."

"We have plant class tonight," I reminded her.

"Tomorrow, then."

"Marlee will be working the memorial party for Wanda."

"Then we'll have a coven meeting during coffee one morning!"

I nodded. "That sounds like a good plan. Who knew it was possible to be too busy for a poltergeist?"

With three more deliveries on my schedule that afternoon, I was grateful for the warm feeling that spread through my body as I sipped on the Cold Hands, Warm Heart potion. Getting goods in and out of the hearse meant I'd be in the biting wind that had kicked up around lunchtime, but I would be well-armed with the potion coursing through me and my full complement of wool coat, knit scarf—the same shade of pink as my magic—and a beanie with the tavern's logo embroidered on it.

Before I could head to my next appointment, though, I ran into Ilya, the man who was claiming to be in town to check out his options for retiring there. I still didn't quite buy it, since the guy was younger than me. I had just reached the back door of the tavern when he waylaid me.

"Oh, hey, hearse lady!" he called.

"Hazel," I supplied.

"Yeah, sorry about that. I couldn't remember your name, and I wanted to catch you before you left." Ilya gave me his off-putting smile. "I hear you turned down the chance to sell your house."

"Oh, has that news made it onto the gossip circuit around town? I guess it's a good thing I didn't sell to Wanda, since she wound up dead."

"How much was she offering?"

I was reminded of the very similar conversation I'd had with Nicole, which had been her attempt at an interview for her newspaper story. Suddenly, I had the wild thought that Ilya might be doing something similar. "Are you an undercover journalist?" I asked.

"Me? No." Ilya gave me a look that he probably thought made him look trustworthy. Instead, it gave me the impression he knew an inside joke but wasn't willing to share it with me. "I'm just a sucker for gossip."

"I figured. After all, you're the one who broke the news about Wanda's death."

"And now there's this mysterious bag of cash. It's all related."

I tilted my head and peered at Ilya closely. "Do you know that for certain, or is it just a guess?"

"Just an educated guess. But how can it not be related? Money is usually a great motivator for murder."

"Hmm" was my only response.

"Your town certainly seems dangerous," Ilya said, gazing around the tavern like he might spot the killer in one of the booths. "It's exciting, but maybe a little too much so, if I'm going to enjoy a quiet retirement here."

"It's not usually like this. I'll be at a magical plant class tonight, over at the Growing Power Garden Store. You should check out local events like that if you're thinking about retiring in Foxfire Haven."

"I might just do that."

I said a hasty goodbye to Ilya and slipped out the back door before he or anyone else could stop me. *Marlee needs to get a read on him,* I thought. If we at least knew what Ilya was feeling underneath that cheerful veneer, we might have an idea of whether or not he was being honest.

By the time I arrived at the garden store that evening, I was cold, hungry, and tired. Valerian's potion had worn off before my last delivery of the day, which wasn't finished until the sun had already disappeared below the line of evergreen-covered hills in the west, and a light rain had begun to fall. I'd gotten home in time to make a quick dinner, so I had pre-heated the oven, then dashed into my bedroom to change into warmer clothes. When I came back into the kitchen, the oven had been turned off. I set the dial again, but nothing happened.

I wasn't sure if the poltergeist had been responsible, or if I was going to have to shell out money to have the old stove repaired. Frankly, I wasn't sure which of those was the best-case scenario. Either way, though, I had already lost time, and I couldn't bake the casserole I had made earlier. It was too big to fit in the microwave, and eventually, I settled for heating up a can of soup on the stovetop. The burners, at least, were still working.

The soup hadn't been quite enough to satisfy me, and as I settled into my spot at the garden store, I wondered if Gnorris had any snacks stashed around the place. *What do gnomes like to snack on, anyway?*

Lenox Williams, Aaron's business partner, came in and started looking around the room.

"I didn't know you were taking this class!" I said, surprised.

"Gnorris talked me into it. That gnome is a good salesman." Lenox gave me a quiet smile, then passed by on her way to a table with a free spot. She would be sharing it with an elf and two other witches.

Gnorris was just walking to the front of the room to begin class when the door opened, and Ilya walked in. His usual grin was plastered across his face as his eyes roved across the room. He spotted me, waved, and began heading in my direction. Meanwhile, I chastised myself for having suggested he check the class out. I just wasn't in the mood to deal with him or his smile.

Since the rest of my coven occupied the other stools at the table, Ilya headed for an empty spot at the table in front of us.

I heard a quiet cry from my right, and I turned to see Lenox slowly raise a finger toward Ilya. Her face was twisted with anger, and I caught a brief spark of magic—the same pale blue hue as her fuzzy sweater—shoot out of her fingertip. "What is that piece of slime doing here?"

Chapter Nineteen

ILYA LOOKED OVER AND gave a start. He rose from his stool, his eyes darting between Lenox and the door.

Lenox's finger was still pointed toward Ilya, and more blue sparks were flying out of it. "If you're here because of me, I have nothing to say!"

Ilya lifted both hands, then made a patting motion. "Calm down. There's no reason to make a scene."

"You're telling me to calm down?" Lenox shot upward, her stool clattering to the floor behind her.

Valerian spread her arms so they were in front of Jo and me. It was like a mom holding out an arm to steady a child after braking too hard in the car. Apparently, she was trying to protect us, in case Lenox's anger created a magical outburst.

"It's okay," Ilya growled. "I'll leave."

"What are you even doing in this town?" Lenox retorted. "First *she* had to turn up here, and now you?"

"Is there a problem?" Gnorris asked. His voice sounded timid and small compared to Lenox's.

Ilya pointed at me, and I jerked backward, like I had been slapped. "I only came here tonight because she said I should."

Lenox shot a glare in my direction, and I mouthed, "Sorry."

Luckily, I escaped Lenox's wrath. "I'm sure Hazel didn't know who she was talking to."

Gnorris had clambered up onto one of the tables, and he clapped his hands several times. "Keep this up, and both of you will be leaving!"

"I'm going," Ilya said. He stalked out of the store.

There was silence as we all sat there, stunned. I was looking at the front door, half-expecting Ilya to come back in for one last retort. Others were staring at Lenox, who huffed out a breath and threw her purse over her shoulder. "Sorry, Gnorris," she muttered as she headed for the door, too.

With neither Ilya nor Lenox there anymore, attention turned to me.

"Who is that guy?" I heard the elf who'd been sitting next to Lenox whisper.

"Hazel invited him?" That came from someone at a table behind me.

I looked at Gnorris, who was still standing on top of the table. "I am so sorry," I told him. "He said he was looking to retire here, and I suggested he check out events around town, like this class, and—"

I broke off when Gnorris waved a hand toward me. "Ah, it's okay. In fact, you might have done me a favor. You know how good a scandal can be for business."

"Glad I could help." I was trying to make a joke, but it came out as an awkward squeak, and a few people in the class laughed. I spotted a lot of shoulders that slowly lowered, and a low buzz emanated through the room as people commented on the bizarre confrontation.

All I knew was that I had been right to be suspicious of Ilya. He wasn't in Foxfire Haven to scout out a town for his future retirement. But that still left some big questions. The first was, of course, why was Ilya really in Foxfire Haven? And, perhaps even more importantly, if he knew Lenox, the business partner of Wanda's ex-husband, then what was his connection to Wanda herself? There was no way Ilya's arrival at almost the same time as Wanda was a coincidence.

There was suddenly a new suspect for Wanda's murder, and I was going to make sure I passed that tip along to Wyatt.

Gnorris clapped his hands again, snapping me out of my thoughts. "Apologies for the bizarre start to our class, folks," he announced. "Let's get back on track, shall we? I was going to talk about plants for money magic tonight, but given what just happened, we're going to focus instead on warding magic, and how the fairy wand plant can help aid spells, potions, and charm bags intended for that. Whether you're trying to ward off negativity or an actual person, this plant can help boost your magical working."

"Oh!" Valerian said in a loud whisper. "That could help us with our poltergeist problem!"

Jo's head snapped toward her. "What poltergeist problem?"

"We'll fill you in," I promised.

Marlee gave me a knowing look. "You learned some more about our mysterious roommate," she said under her breath.

I nodded, then decided to do my best imitation of Jo. I didn't carry a notebook around, like she did, but

I put my cell phone on the table and opened up the note-taking app. I was going to write down everything Gnorris taught us about warding magic, in case it would be useful for keeping the paranormal activity at home at an acceptable level.

All four of us paid close attention to Gnorris as he lectured us about fairy wand, including tips for harvesting the seeds and how to store them. When it came time for us to try our hand at cutting the leaves properly for spells and potions, I was happy to see not one of us mangled our plants.

It was during that part of the class that Marlee said, "Jo, we've had so much going on that we forgot to ask you how the meeting with your editor went. Did Sam tell you what you were hoping to hear?"

Jo beamed. "Yes, actually! Sam does want me to take over the newspaper someday. He wants to retire in the next couple of years, and he said this business with Wanda only reinforced his desire for a quieter life. He's going to start training me on the business side of things, so I'm ready to handle it all myself when the day comes."

"Jo! That's fantastic!" I enthused.

Marlee reached over and high-fived Jo. "You manifested that!"

"And we're going to celebrate it!" Valerian declared. "I'll buy a round at the tavern after class!"

"You're only offering because you get an employee discount," Jo teased.

"Oh, no, I can't go!" Marlee held up a hand and wiggled three fingers. "I've got three tasks I have to wrap up tonight if I'm going to pull off that memorial party tomorrow."

"Then how about I make us drinks at home?" Valerian suggested. "That way, you can get started on your work while you sip."

"Done!"

"Now," Jo said, her smile slipping, "what's this about a poltergeist problem?"

"We apparently have another ghost," I explained. "It's one who likes to move things. And by move, I mean throw."

There wasn't a hint of sarcasm when Jo said, "Oh, good."

Jo's response was not what any of us had expected, and we all gave her an incredulous look. She tugged on a stalk of the fairy wand in front of her. "Two weeks ago, I walked into my room to find all of my plants had been rearranged. I actually wondered if I'd had some kind of sleepwalking incident and done it myself. I also considered someone had broken into my room just so they could redecorate. The idea that a ghost did it is much more comforting."

"A redecorating intruder?" I asked with a laugh. "Can you please find one of those who would like to tackle my bedroom? I could really use some help in there."

We wrapped up the class in high spirits, despite the very uncomfortable start to the evening. Even Gnorris was smiling contentedly as we wished him a good night. "How long until my store is being talked about at the tavern?" he asked Valerian with a wink. "I'm going to have to pay Hazel for the free marketing!"

Marlee had driven me to plant class that night, and we chatted happily on the drive home. She was anxious to keep checking things off her to-do list for the party, but she was also feeling good after an evening with her coven.

When Marlee turned into our driveway, I spotted someone standing on the front porch.

At this point, I should expect to find someone waiting every time I come home.

There was no rental car parked out front, but I immediately thought of Nicole. Was she coming to pay us yet another visit?

But, as we got closer, it was obvious it was a man standing there, and he was much taller than Nicole.

It was Wyatt. He must have walked over from his house.

"What is he doing here?" Marlee asked as she pulled to a stop.

"I was thinking the same thing." I got out of the car slowly, steeling myself for whatever was about to come, when I heard Marlee's raised voice.

"Jo didn't murder anyone!" she shouted. Marlee was usually the more temperate one, and I was shocked to hear her defensive tone. "Don't tell me you've come back to—oh! Oh, that's not why you're here. You're feeling..." Marlee turned and gave me a helpless look.

"Hi, Wyatt," I called. "What can we do for you?"

"I need a word with you, Hazel."

Chapter Twenty

"Come on in," I told Wyatt. I quickly moved up the porch steps, unlocked the door, and led the way to the living room. Wyatt followed me, but Marlee stayed on the front porch. I figured she was going to stay there to let Jo and Valerian know about our visitor as soon as they got home. They had both been getting into their cars when Marlee and I had left the garden store.

I shut the living room door once Wyatt and I were inside. Briefly, I considered offering him a cup of tea, but the last time I'd done that, we'd only wound up arguing. Instead, I gestured toward the sofa while I settled into a chair.

Wyatt usually looked at me with one of two expressions: annoyance or resignation. At the moment, though, he wasn't looking at me at all. He was staring down at his hands, which were clasped together tightly. I noticed the shimmer of raindrops in his silver hair. He had definitely walked from his house a few doors down.

The silence was beginning to get uncomfortable when Wyatt finally looked at me. "I owe you an apology. I'm sorry I asked you to keep an eye on Ms. Davenport. I should know better than to ask a witch to do something like that to a member of her own coven."

I opened my mouth to say thanks, but there was something about Wyatt's tense shoulders that stopped me. He wasn't done yet, I could tell.

I could also tell my magic was starting to build up. Even in this moment, when Wyatt was being apologetic instead of grumpy, he was still triggering a rise in my magic.

"My wife was a solitary witch," he said quietly, "but she told me what it was like to be in a coven, how strong the bond is between the witches in it."

I nodded, thinking of the bond I had with my own coven. Jo, Marlee, and Valerian had become like sisters to me. I was also curious about Wyatt's wife. He had mentioned Constance to me once before, and all I knew was that she had died. I had gotten the impression then that Wyatt didn't talk about her often. At least, not with people like me, whom he wasn't close with.

"I appreciate the apology," I said sincerely. Then, hesitantly, I added, "How long has Constance been gone?"

"Nine years now." There was no hesitation in his voice, which meant he didn't have to stop and think how long he'd been without her. I wasn't an empath like Marlee, but I could almost feel his pain. "Crazy thing is that it wasn't the cancer that killed her. It was the magical treatment she tried. She said she might as well give it a shot since her days were numbered anyway, but—"

Wyatt broke off and looked down at his hands again. Without thinking what I was doing, I got up and moved to sit down next to him on the couch. I put my hand on his back, much like Barry had done to me at the tavern. "I'm so sorry," I said. My voice cracked, and I bit my lip in an effort to hold back the tears I felt forming.

"Ms. Davenport was a long shot, anyway," Wyatt said. He clearly wanted to move on to a different subject.

"Of course she was. Do you know that guy Ilya who showed up in town about the same time as Wanda and Nicole?"

Wyatt quickly swiped the back of a hand against his cheek, then gave me a curious look. "No. Who is this person?"

I described Ilya, from his giant, creepy smile to his claim about why he was in Foxfire Haven. Then, I gave Wyatt a blow-by-blow account of the scene between Ilya and Lenox that night. I ended with, "Gnorris figures he'll sell a few extra plants from the free marketing the story will provide."

Wyatt chuckled. "That little gnome is a clever businessman. And thank you for the tip. I've seen a guy matching that description, but people are always in and out of this town, touring magical spots or visiting family. I hadn't considered he might be involved in this case."

"I hope he leaves soon," I said, more to myself than to Wyatt.

"Glad it's not me who's on your bad side at the moment." Wyatt gave me a teasing look.

"Let's keep it that way."

"In other words, I should head home before we stop being nice to each other." Wyatt stood. "Please pass my apology on to the others, as well."

"I will. Thank you." I walked Wyatt out, wished him a good night, then wandered into the kitchen. I felt like I was in a bit of a daze from the unexpected conversation. I'd learned more about Wyatt's late wife and, more importantly, he'd apologized to me.

Perkins and Stella were crammed into the nest I'd made from strips of old flannel pajamas, and Perkins lifted his head and made a cooing sound that seemed to end in a question mark.

"I'm okay, Perky," I assured him as I made a beeline for the kettle.

"First of all," Valerian said from her perch at the table, where she was slicing limes, "don't bother with tea, because we're about to have that celebratory cocktail for Jo. Second, I'm no empath, but I can feel your sadness."

"Me, too." Marlee pressed a hand against her chest. "It's deep, like an ache in your soul."

I gave myself a good shake and saw the pink sparks that fluttered to the floor. "It's not my sadness. Wyatt was talking about his late wife. She died of cancer."

Jo, who was pulling glasses out of the cupboard, glanced over at me. "He came over here to talk about her?"

"No, he came to apologize for asking me to keep an eye on you, and he asked me to pass along his apology. He knows it was wrong to ask me to go against someone in my coven."

"Good man," Valerian said. "Marlee, grab the spiced rum, please. Hazel, you march outside, right now, and shed all that excess magic. I'm not going to make four amazing cocktails, only to have you knock them all over with your magic."

"That would be a shame." I was still in my coat, so I followed Valerian's orders immediately. Perkins reluctantly joined me, perching on my shoulder and making little noises that were, I was certain, his way of complaining about the cold.

There was a small puddle of magic in the middle of the backyard by the time I came back inside. By then, Valerian was handing around the glasses, and I slid out of my coat, then accepted mine.

"To Jo Davenport, future editor and publisher of the *Foxfire Haven Recorder*!" Marlee said, raising her glass.

We all raised ours in return, then took a sip. It tasted like sitting on a tropical beach: warm, refreshing, and with just a hint of saltiness. "Oh, Val," I moaned contentedly.

"Yes, what Hazel said." Jo took another long sip, her eyes closed. "We need something to celebrate at least once a week, so we have an excuse to drink these."

That night, I dreamed of walking along a white sandy beach while listening to the rhythm of waves coming into shore. My alarm clock woke me up right as I was about to wade into the water. Valerian had infused some sort of magic into that cocktail.

What I needed more than good dreams, though, was energy. By lunchtime, all I wanted to do was go back to bed for a nap. I had already made four runs in the hearse for the party that night. It had taken two trips to get the rest of the decorations shuttled over from the party supply store in Stanton, and then, I'd had to pick up cupcakes from The Salt Circle, and I had retrieved a custom banner from the print shop.

At least all this running around will be done by seven o'clock tonight, I told myself. That was when the party started, and if something had yet to be delivered at that time, then it just wasn't going to happen. I was on the home stretch.

I had only one more delivery to make after I hastily ate a sandwich and potato salad at the breakfast table. Marlee had purposely left most of my afternoon open, in case she needed me to make any last-minute runs.

There was a barbecue restaurant on the far Western side of Foxfire Haven that would be providing some of the food for the party that night. Flying High Barbecue was housed in a ramshackle building nestled in a cluster of evergreen trees just off a narrow two-lane road. It was the kind of place no one would just stumble on: either you knew it was there, or you didn't. Luckily for the owners, plenty of people knew it was there. A line was snaking out the door when I walked up.

I hadn't been to Flying High Barbecue since I was a teenager, but the place didn't look like it had changed much. I was happily surprised when I saw Garth standing behind a large barbecue positioned to one side of the restaurant. He was turning over a giant hunk of meat, and despite having just eaten lunch, the scent of barbecue made my stomach growl.

"Hi!" I called to the gargoyle. "I saw you at the tavern last weekend. I'm Hazel, Marlee's roommate."

Garth's face lit up, and he put down the tongs he was using—which were oversized to fit his hands better—to give me a fist bump. "Hazel, hi! I saw you pull up in the hearse. I've heard of Dead Easy Delivery, but this is the first time I've gotten to see you in action."

"This is your place now?" I asked.

"My family's." Garth looked around proudly. "My grandfather started this restaurant nearly fifty years ago.

My brother manages it these days, I make sure everything tastes great, and my sister gets out and lets the magical world know we're here."

I jerked my head in the direction of the line. "I'd say she's doing a great job of that." I leaned toward the grill and made a show of sniffing. "The pulled pork I'm here to pick up might not make it until the party tonight."

"Don't worry, I'll send you home with a plate of food for yourself. No need to dip into Marlee's stash." Garth paused, then added, "This is the first time she's used us for one of her events. You know, I didn't ask her out to get her business."

"It never occurred to me that you did. The two of you seemed to hit it off at the tavern."

"Yeah, I'm looking forward to getting to know her better. In the meantime, let me grab my brother. He'll help you load up."

"I'll go grab the gurney."

Garth grinned. "A gurney? This just gets better and better."

The brother, as it turned out, was a full head taller than Garth. Garrett singlehandedly loaded everything onto the gurney, then slid it into the hearse for me. And "singlehandedly" was literal, in this case. One of Garrett's hands was holding his cell phone to his ear the entire time.

The next time I needed help hauling heavy stuff, I would check to see if the gargoyles ever did freelance work.

As his brother had promised, Garrett handed me a small piece of paper once we were done. It was a coupon for a meal on the house, and he escorted me to the front of the line. A few people gave me sour looks, but Garrett explained I was delivering barbecue for that night's memorial, and that time was of the essence. There was clearly no need to explain what memorial he was referring to, because I heard Wanda's name several times as people began to murmur.

I was on my way out, a Styrofoam container in my hands, when I spotted Wanda's ex-husband, Aaron, in the line.

"Hey," I said, stepping close so the people around him wouldn't be able to hear us. "How are you doing?"

"Okay, I guess." Aaron began to wind a finger around the cord of his sweatshirt's hood. "I'm still trying to accept that Wanda is gone. One minute I was ready to give her money, and the next, she was dead."

CHAPTER TWENTY-ONE

I SHIFTED THE FOOD container so I could move even closer to Aaron. "What do you mean, you were ready to give Wanda money?"

Had the bag of cash belonged to Aaron?

"She came over to see me the night before she died," Aaron said. He looked sheepish about it, which was no surprise since he had been roundly criticizing her so shortly before her visit to his house.

"I know," I admitted.

"Well, she talked me into investing in the newspaper." Aaron dipped his head, looking even more ashamed of himself.

His head whipped up in surprise when I nearly shouted, "Ah-ha!" I clamped my lips together, waited for the startled people in line around us to stop looking at me, then continued in a quieter voice, "Then it was *your* bag of cash we found behind the tavern!"

It was Aaron's turn to surprise me, because he laughed. "Of course not! I was going to transfer the money from my bank account to hers, so it was all above board. I'm a businessman, not the mafia."

So much for that lead.

"I'm surprised Lenox didn't try to talk you out of it," I said.

"Oh, she was furious when I admitted it to her. Luckily, Wanda was dead by the next day, so Lenox soon knew my money wasn't going anywhere. She's forgiven me."

Using the word "luckily" in the same breath as mentioning his ex-wife's murder wasn't the best choice for someone who didn't want to look like a suspect. Instead of pointing that out to Aaron, though, I mentioned that I'd witnessed the run-in between Lenox and Ilya at the garden store.

Aaron grimaced. "I heard all about it, at top volume. Lenox is so upset that Ilya is in town, not to mention that he showed up at the class. She's also really embarrassed about making such a big scene."

"Who is Ilya? He's clearly been hiding his real purpose for being in Foxfire Haven."

"I don't know why he's here for certain, but I think it's safe to say he was working for Wanda. He's been doing her dirty work for a long time now."

"Dirty work?" I repeated. It had never occurred to me Ilya had been working with Wanda. If anything, I would have guessed he was after her or her money.

"Ilya is a private investigator. When Wanda and I were getting divorced, she hired him to find out if I was using my new business to hide money from her. Instead, he caught Lenox in a scandal. It was an old financial scheme she'd gotten tangled up in, and she'd worked really hard to move on from it. Ilya's findings brought it all crashing back and nearly ruined her reputation. And our brand-new business, for that matter."

Lenox Williams was suddenly at the top of my suspect list. Had she killed Wanda to get revenge for exposing her all those years ago in Florida? Maybe Lenox had spotted Ilya in town and decided to get rid of Wanda once and for all, before she could have Ilya dig up any more embarrassing history.

"No wonder she got upset when Ilya waltzed into class," I mused. And that, I reminded myself, was totally my fault.

"I told her she was unlikely to be his target this time around." Aaron shuffled forward as the line moved, and I did a crab-walk to keep my spot next to him. "I think it's much more likely he was here to dig up information on Sam Doane. If Wanda could find something bad in his record, she could have blackmailed him into accepting a lowball offer for the newspaper."

I gave a low whistle. "She was a real piece of work."

"I'm still trying to figure out why I ever married her."

"Now that Ilya is no longer working for Wanda, why is he still in town?"

"Not my business." Aaron said it dismissively, but then, a small smile grew on his face. "But I hope it's because he's a suspect, and the constables asked him not to leave town until this is all sorted out. I love the idea of him being on the receiving end of the scrutiny."

"And I do hope it's all sorted out soon. Thank you for the information, Aaron. And, now, I've got to get going while this barbecue is still hot."

I had been referring to the Styrofoam coolers full of steaming barbecue inside the hearse, but I also meant my own food. In addition to the pulled pork, I had a big pile of macaroni and cheese plus baked beans waiting for me. It all smelled delicious.

First, though, I had a delivery to make. I got the food to the community center and handed it off to the person Marlee had hired to oversee the food and beverages that evening. Then, I sat down at one of the tables already set up for the party and dug into my food.

It tasted even better than it had smelled. I didn't stop eating until I was so full I felt like I was going to roll right off the chair.

Once my stomach was satisfied, I had another important piece of business to attend to. After what I'd passed along to Wyatt about Ilya and his confrontation with Lenox, I expected he or another constable had already had a chat with Mr. I'm Just Researching Places for Retirement.

Ilya could have come up with a better excuse than that, surely. Weren't private investigators supposed to be really good at adopting personas? Or was I basing that assumption off every P.I. TV show I'd ever seen?

Even though I had told myself, several times, that Wyatt and the constables had things under control, I called Wyatt, anyway, to tell him about my conversation with Aaron.

Or, at least, I tried. I got his voicemail, so I wound up leaving an overly long and rambling message about having some information to share. I hung up feeling a little silly, but with that done, I headed home to rest a bit before the party that night. I didn't have to be there, since I'd been hired for deliveries, not to attend, but I wanted to support Marlee.

And, yes, if I were being honest, I also wanted to be there to observe people. I knew Nicole would attend, and I was hoping both Ilya and Aaron would put in appearances. If I could just get some more information about any of them, it might help me home in on who the real killer was.

As usual, I tried telling myself it was none of my business, but between Wanda pushing me around about selling my home and the constables eyeballing Jo, I wanted to have the whole thing over and done with.

Maybe I should try that same spell Aaron wanted to do. What had it been called? A Lay it to Rest spell.

Ten minutes after I got home, I was in the kitchen, scratching Perkins on the head, when I caught a blur of red in my peripheral vision. It was followed by a loud crash, and I looked over to see a coffee mug on the floor. It had broken in half, and since it was a Christmas mug, Santa Claus's face had taken the worst of the damage.

I want to lay this poltergeist to rest.

After cleaning up the shards of the mug, I was debating taking a quick snooze on the couch or staying alert to any more paranormal activity when Wyatt called me back.

"Your voicemail didn't make a lot of sense," Wyatt began.

"Yeah, sorry about that. It's about Ilya, that new guy in town. He's a private investigator, and he was probably working for Wanda."

There was silence on the other end of the line, and I pictured Wyatt staring out the window of his office, mulling over that tidbit. "We know he's a P.I., but what makes you think he was here to do work for Wanda?"

I recounted everything Aaron had told me, though I left out the part about Lenox and her financial embarrassment. Aaron had said she worked hard to leave it behind, and I wasn't going to dredge it up.

Wyatt thanked me for the details, then told me I could have waited to pass along the information that night, at the party. "I'm sure half the town will turn out, including you and me."

"Yeah, I'll be there. I want to support Marlee, since she's organizing the whole thing."

"Mm-hmm, I'm sure that's why you're going." I could almost hear Wyatt's sly smile.

"I'll see you there," I promised.

But first, I definitely needed to be horizontal for a while. I stretched out on the couch, and the poltergeist would have had to throw something straight at my head to make me stir. Perkins even settled into the crook of my elbow to nap with me.

I felt refreshed after that, though I was in danger of using all my newfound energy to choose an outfit. What was one supposed to wear to a memorial party for a murdered woman who was generally disliked by everyone? Somber black would make it seem too much like a funeral, but a little black dress might put too much emphasis on the "party" aspect.

Eventually, I opted for a black wool skirt that looked great with a pair of tall black leather boots. To keep from looking like I was in mourning, though, I paired the skirt with a purple and white floral blouse topped with a purple cardigan. I looked serious but not sad.

Wyatt had said half the town would probably be at the memorial for Wanda, and as I cruised down Main Street in the hearse, I realized he had been right. There wasn't an open parking spot anywhere along the street, and a dirt lot one street over was already full.

Eventually, I wound up finding a parking spot on a street full of gorgeous Victorian houses. It was a five-minute walk to the community center from there, and I realized that between the walk and the amount of time I'd driven around looking for parking, I could have walked or bicycled from home and been there already.

When I walked inside the community center, the first thing I noticed was the decor. The framed newspaper pages on loan from the library were displayed on a table covered with a dark-blue cloth, and there were huge flower arrangements on the tables that looked like a cross between funeral flowers and something more fit for a celebration. In all, I felt like Marlee had managed to pull off the right balance between a memorial and a party.

The second thing I noticed once I got inside wasn't a thing at all. It was a person. Mayor Euphoria Lachlan was standing in front of the food table, and I heard her say, "Don't they have anything that's low-fat?"

I turned and walked in the opposite direction from Euphoria, since I had no interest in running into my old high-school bully. If Euphoria ever had something nice to say to me, I would probably also spot a pig flying over my house on the same day.

I headed toward Marlee, who was talking to Jo and Sam next to a big book for people to write messages in. "Who's the book for?" I asked.

"Nicole," Marlee said. "We thought she'd like to take home a memento of her boss's impact on the Foxfire Haven community."

I sure hoped people were choosing to be polite rather than truthful as they penned their messages.

"She'll be sticking a tape recorder in your face later," Jo warned me. "She's trying to get quotes from everyone who met Wanda."

"Again?" I asked.

"I told her she could write a story about the memorial," Sam said. He gave me a look that said he was doing it to be nice, and I nodded in understanding.

"I'm going to find the dessert table," I announced. After my free barbecue, I figured I had just enough room for a cupcake.

In addition to dessert, I also found a few people I knew from around town. I caught up with Stacy from the stationery shop, Sable—an elf who made incredible magical fireworks—stopped to say hello, and I even had a brief chat with Newton Yates, a werefrog who was still gunning for one of the vacant city council spots.

I knew that because Newton talked about nothing but how I should vote for him. The election to fill the two vacant spots was scheduled for the following month, and I couldn't wait for it to be over.

When my watch said it was nearly nine o'clock, I started thinking about slipping out and heading home for some peace and quiet. I wanted to check in with Marlee first, but I couldn't find her anywhere.

Once two laps around the room failed to turn up my roommate, I headed down a long hallway that led to the bathrooms. When I reached the ladies' room door,

I heard raised voices coming from somewhere ahead of me.

Two people were arguing around the corner, where another hallway met the one I was in. I immediately recognized Sam's voice, but I couldn't make out his words.

I could, however, hear Nicole's response to him clearly. "I don't have the money, anyway, so I guess it doesn't matter!"

CHAPTER TWENTY-TWO

MY MIND WAS RACING so quickly I actually reached up and clutched my head with both hands. It felt like my brain was going to burst right out of me. What money was Nicole talking about? And if she didn't have it, did that mean it was because she was referring to the bag of cash that we'd turned in to the constables?

I heard the distinct click of high heels, followed by a loud voice. "Hazel Underwood, are you spying on people?"

I spun around to find myself face-to-face with the mayor. I had managed to avoid Euphoria all night long, and she had caught me at the worst possible moment. Behind her, the door of the ladies' room was slowly swinging closed. She'd come out and caught me eavesdropping on Sam and Nicole.

"Hazel, what's going on?" It was Sam's voice.

"She's listening in on your private conversation, of course." Euphoria gave me a smirk, then turned and clicked away on her silver heels.

I clenched my jaw, thinking very unkind thoughts about Euphoria, then forced my face to relax enough so I could explain myself to Sam without looking guilty.

Sam didn't seem angry, at least. Instead, he simply looked curious.

Also, he did not look surprised at all, and I wondered how much Jo had told him about my tendency to insert myself into murder cases.

Nicole, on the other hand, had a red face, and there were tears slowly rolling down her cheeks. She took two steps toward me, then jammed a finger toward my face, its tip just inches from my nose. "This is all her fault!"

"What's my fault?" I asked as I stepped backward to put some distance between my nose and her accusatory finger.

"Not you! I mean the writer in your coven. Josephine." Nicole said her name like it was a curse. She lowered her arm, and both of her hands curled into fists. Then, she let out a shrill shriek of frustration. "I just can't get ahead, no matter how hard I try!"

I barely had time to jump out of the way to avoid being slammed in the shoulder as Nicole stalked past me. I watched her for a few seconds, then turned back to Sam. "I'm so sorry. I was looking for Marlee, and I heard you two arguing. Why is she so upset about Jo?"

"Nicole offered to buy out the newspaper since Wanda is no longer able to do it," Sam said. He sounded tired and sad. "I told her I wasn't selling out to anybody, because the newspaper will be Jo's someday."

"That's what she meant about money. She had her hands on funding but lost it somehow."

"I suppose. She made her pitch to me, I said no, and she left my office in a huff. That was the day after Wanda's murder. We never talked about money, or how much I would want if I was willing to sell."

There were firm footfalls behind me, coming from the direction of the party. I knew without looking it was Wyatt, and I breathed a sigh of relief that it wasn't Euphoria coming back to cause more trouble.

"What's going on? The mayor said there's trouble brewing down here."

Yeah, because she brewed it.

"The trouble just stomped away," Sam said. He ran a hand across his face. "Wanda is dead, but she continues to make my life difficult even from beyond the grave."

"Beyond the morgue, really," Wyatt said affably. "Her funeral and burial will be back in Florida."

"Should we be worried about Jo?" I asked Sam. "I don't want Nicole to go after her."

"Ms. Davenport?" Wyatt's tone turned serious in an instant. "Is she in danger?"

Sam told him what Nicole had said about her inability to buy the paper being Jo's fault.

"But if Nicole no longer has the money to make an offer," I said, "then being mad at Jo is pointless."

"She lost some money, huh? And you think she lost it out behind the tavern, don't you?" Wyatt was looking at me without a trace of teasing. He had made the same connection, and he wasn't discounting it as a good theory.

I nodded. "It's certainly a possibility, but where would Nicole have gotten that much cash to begin with?"

"Maybe it was Wanda's," Sam guessed. "When she died, Nicole could have scooped up anything she had of value."

I sucked in my breath. "Oh! She did mention that she had a key to Wanda's room!"

"She denied knowing anything about that bag when we asked her about it, but I guess it's worth a second try." Wyatt glanced at his watch. "We'll call her down to the station tomorrow morning. Sam, you okay?"

"Yeah. Just ready to get past all this. Here I thought throwing a memorial party would provide some closure." Sam reached out and squeezed my shoulder. "I'm going to stick close to Jo whenever you ladies aren't with her. Just in case Nicole isn't done yet."

"Thanks."

As soon as Sam was gone, I turned to Wyatt. "Whatever Euphoria said about me is untrue. Well, it probably is true, because yes, I was listening in on Sam and Nicole arguing, but I couldn't help but hear them, and I really was just coming down here to find Marlee, and—"

Wyatt suddenly grabbed my hand, and I was so startled I immediately stopped talking.

He lifted my hand until it was nearly even with my face. "You might want to do something about this."

There was a pink halo around my entire hand, and I knew my arm probably had the same glow underneath my cardigan. I glanced down and saw a bare trace of magic pooled at my feet. I'd had a magical exhalation, and I hadn't even noticed. That was not good. It was frustrating enough to shed my magic unintentionally, but it was worse when I didn't even realize it was happening.

Wyatt dropped my hand, and I gave it a good shake. The magic sticking to it sloughed off and drifted down to join the rest of the pile.

"I was going to go home," I said, almost like it explained my situation. "Now I feel like I need to stay for Jo."

"Right now, you need to get rid of all that magic. But I'm not letting you wander off alone, because the last thing I need is for Nicole to find you again and trigger one of your infamous magical outbursts."

"They are not infamous," I countered, feeling embarrassed. "I'll go around the corner and do a quick shedding spell to get rid of anything that's left inside me."

At least Wyatt stayed where he was, so I had some privacy as I said the incantation for releasing my magic. I felt like a kid who was too irresponsible to be left without a babysitter. A tall, silver-haired, grumpy babysitter.

A bit more magic puffed out from my body as I said the incantation, and once it had drifted to the floor and mostly dissipated, I rejoined Wyatt. "All set," I told him.

"Good, because I'm starving. I'm going to go get some pulled pork before it's all gone."

"Have some of the mac and cheese, too," I advised.

Wyatt and I both began walking back in the direction of the party, but I slowed my pace and let him move ahead on his own while I resumed my search for Marlee. She had to be there somewhere.

Finally, I spotted Marlee's black ponytail over by the makeshift bar. Valerian was working, thanks to a deal Marlee had worked out with the tavern. The tavern owner figured no one would be at Sit a Spell that night, anyway, so he had agreed to run the bar at the party.

"Where have you been?" I asked as I came to a stop next to Marlee. "Sorry. That came out kind of harsh."

Marlee snaked an arm through mine. "I was out back, taking a break. You, however, have been neck-deep in some drama. I can feel your frustration."

I waited until Valerian was close to us, and I motioned for her to lean in over the folding table that was serving as a bar. Quickly, I told her and Marlee about the confrontation between Sam and Nicole, and Nicole's resentment toward Jo.

"I should go find Nicole and see what she's feeling right now," Marlee said. She began looking around the room, but when her eyes lit up, I knew it wasn't Nicole she had seen.

Instead, it was Jo. Sam was at her elbow, and I was grateful he'd made good on his promise to keep an eye on her.

Sam met my gaze, and he raised his eyebrows in a questioning sort of look. I took it to be his way of asking *You've got her?* I nodded, and Sam walked off after saying something quietly to Jo.

"Jo, did Sam tell you about Nicole?" Marlee asked.

"Yeah." Jo sounded weary, and she briefly leaned against me. "Is it bedtime yet?"

"Go home and get some sleep!" Marlee made a shooing motion at Jo. "I'm only here because Sam is paying me to run this party."

"I might join you," I told Jo. "This night just keeps getting weirder."

Valerian used the empty beer bottle in her hand like a pointer as she stretched her arm out to her right. "And it just got even more weird. Look!"

The rest of us turned to see Aaron stalking up to Ilya. Aaron's cheeks were red, either from anger or too much alcohol. As we watched, Ilya seemed to finally notice he was being approached, and he took a step backward as his hands came up in a defensive stance.

It was too late, though. Aaron was still striding forward when he pulled his right arm back and punched Ilya right in the face.

CHAPTER TWENTY-THREE

THE ROOM ERUPTED INTO chaos. Some people dashed forward to help Ilya, who had landed flat on his back, while a couple more took Aaron by the arms. Everyone else was doing some combination of staring, pointing, or shouting.

Above the din, though, I heard a sharp cry behind me. I looked over my shoulder to see Nicole. She was just a few feet away from Jo, and I instinctively wrapped my arm around Jo's waist and pulled her in front of me. I didn't want to bear the brunt of Nicole's wrath again, but I'd rather it be me than Jo.

Marlee was staring at Nicole, her face pale. Her breathing was rapid, and she swayed a bit on her feet.

"There are too many strong emotions in here!" Jo yelled. "She's gonna crash!"

Jo and I both reached out to steady Marlee, and I distantly heard Valerian tell someone, "Take over. I'll be back."

The three of us led Marlee to a chair in the corner, and although she was still in the same room as everyone else, she was, at least, farther away from Aaron, Ilya, and even Nicole.

Valerian began to say the words of what I recognized as a shielding spell to protect Marlee's energy. Jo and I joined hands with her and added our voices as Valerian began to repeat the words.

Marlee was still pale, her head thrown back and her eyes shut tightly. Her arms hung limply at her sides, and for a moment, I worried she had passed out. I was relieved, then, when she croaked, "I'm okay."

"You are not okay," Jo said, breaking off the spell.

"Well, I will be." Marlee groaned. "I'm supposed to be organizing this event, not falling apart at it."

"Was it Nicole who sent you over the edge?" I asked.

Marlee opened her eyes and rolled her head around in a stretch, then returned to a normal sitting position. "It's been building all night. People have such conflicting feelings about this event. They didn't like Wanda, they're curious about her murder, and they're having fun hanging out with friends, all at the same time. That kind of confusion can really get to me. Add in the fact that I've been stressed about planning a whole event in such a short time, and I couldn't stop all the anger I felt coming from both Nicole and Wanda's ex."

"Well," I said with a shaky laugh, "you did say you wanted to get a read on her emotions."

"And I did, all right! So much anger and resentment. But there was something else, too. A sort of sadness."

"Her boss did just get murdered," Jo pointed out. "She hasn't been acting like someone who's grieving, but that could just be a mask."

"Whatever she's sad about, it's not as strong of a feeling as her anger." Marlee looked at Valerian. "Can I please have something to drink?"

"You want a gin and tonic? The angelica root in gin is really good for calming the mind."

Marlee shook her head. "I meant something a little more sedate, like water."

"But I'll take a gin and tonic," Jo said.

Valerian moved off to get the drinks while Jo and I kept watch over Marlee. She was looking better by the minute, but I kept my focus on maintaining the magical shield Valerian had built up around us. I silently repeated the spell in my head.

Five minutes later, Valerian came back with a glass of water for Marlee. There were three gin and tonics on the tray. "I figured we could all use the calming," she quipped as she handed glasses around, then took the last one for herself. "By the way, I heard something interesting while I was making these."

Valerian paused, and Jo made an impatient *go-ahead* motion with her hand. "Out with it, Val!"

"Someone standing near Ilya overheard Aaron just before he let his fist do the talking for him. He said something to Ilya about it not being blackmail, then added, 'Besides, it was supposed to be anonymous!'"

"What isn't blackmail?" Jo asked. She wedged her drink in the crook of her arm so she could pull out her notebook and pen. She had snapped into reporter mode.

"That's all I know," Valerian said.

"I think I can fill in some blanks," I offered. "I ran into Aaron at Flying High Barbecue earlier—by the way, Marlee, Garth is really excited to take you out—and he told me that Wanda had talked him into investing in the newspaper, if she was able to get Sam to agree to the deal. I wonder if Ilya thought she was blackmailing him into doing it?"

"Poor guy," Valerian said. "His ex-wife isn't even alive anymore, and she's still causing problems for him."

"Sam said almost exactly the same thing about her just a few minutes ago, but at least he didn't get into a fight about her. I wonder if Aaron has been arrested for slugging Ilya."

"I'm sorry," Jo said, her notebook forgotten for the moment, "but, Val, did you just call Aaron a poor guy? Let's not forget that he's a suspect. He's not a poor guy if he killed Wanda!"

"He didn't kill Wanda. You did!"

We all turned to see Nicole staring Jo down. Her expression was even angrier than it had been when she'd shouted at me earlier.

"We know you're upset about Wanda's murder," Valerian said in a kind but firm tone, "but running around shouting accusations at people isn't helpful."

Nicole spared Valerian a glare before returning her attention to Jo. "I'll accuse anyone I want. Why shouldn't I? She's the reason Wanda is dead!"

I sighed and pinched the bridge of my nose. "You seemed so nice when we first met."

Once again, I found myself the subject of Nicole's ferocity. "That was before you witches ruined everything!"

"What did we ruin?" Marlee asked. She still looked a bit unsteady as she rose from her chair, but there was also a look of defiance on her face. Her coven was being threatened, and she wasn't going to take it sitting down.

"You say 'witches' like it's a bad thing," Valerian said. Of the four of us, she was the only one who seemed completely unruffled by the whole scene.

Instead of answering, Nicole threw the glass in her hand toward Valerian. The clear liquid inside splashed up into Valerian's face as she fumbled to catch the glass, but it slipped right out of her grasp and fell to the floor. I heard the sound of it shattering as I watched Nicole lunge toward Jo, her fingers bent like claws.

Before I could react, Nicole froze. Her entire body stopped in a sort of half-jump, and only her fingers moved as she tried to get her fingernails closer to Jo's face.

Barry had grabbed Nicole from behind, one hand on her shoulder and the other grasping the back of her short black jacket.

I'd seen Barry sad and brooding. I'd seen him laugh. I'd also seen him being thoughtful as he reminisced about Uncle Grant.

But I had never seen Barry angry. It was utterly terrifying. His expression hadn't changed much from what it usually was. Rather, it was his stance and his energy that gave off a feeling of danger. I had to force myself not to shrink back from him, and I reminded myself that neither I nor the members of my coven were in any danger from him. Barry was on our side.

His eyes were on Jo, and I suddenly understood he wasn't on our side, at all. He was on hers.

When Barry spoke, his tone was gentle, but the feeling of danger persisted. "Is this woman bothering you, Josie?"

CHAPTER TWENTY-FOUR

BEFORE JO COULD ANSWER Barry, Wyatt walked up. We must have made a bizarre tableau, with Nicole's fingers still outstretched to claw at Jo, a Bigfoot holding her back, Marlee swaying like she was slightly drunk, and Valerian wiping liquid off her face with a cocktail napkin.

Barry turned calmly to Wyatt. "She was trying to attack Jo."

"Because she killed Wanda!" Nicole spat.

Wyatt's tone was as serene as Barry's. "Do you have proof of that, Ms. Murrow?"

Nicole's hands moved so she was pointing at both Marlee and Jo with one, and Valerian and me with the other. "She even got them involved! You think they really found that cash by accident? Jo stole it from Wanda and gave it to them out there behind the tavern!"

"Really?" Wyatt's eyes narrowed. "If that's the case, then why did these ladies turn the cash in to me? I've been inside Hazel's funeral home, and trust me, they could have used that money."

Nicole looked panicked for a moment, and when she continued, a note of hesitance had crept into her voice.

"Maybe they were scared of getting caught, and they bailed on the plan. By pretending they had found the bag, they could claim they were helping out. It's a great way for them to look squeaky-clean."

Wyatt glanced at me. "The next time there's a party in this town, I'm not coming. I recommend you stay home, too."

"Deal."

"Ms. Davenport, would you like to press charges for assault?"

Jo looked at Nicole for so long she began to squirm uncomfortably. Since she was still in Barry's grip, it looked slightly comical. Still, I couldn't imagine what it must feel like to have a Bigfoot at your back and an offended witch staring you down.

Finally, though, Jo's expression relaxed. "She didn't manage to get to me, thanks to Barry. I'm not going to press charges. I expect Nicole has been through enough this week."

"You sure?" Barry asked.

When Jo nodded, Barry very slowly let go of Nicole, one hand at a time. She didn't show any signs of going after Jo again, and he took a step back to give her a little breathing room.

"Let's go," Wyatt said to Nicole.

"You can't arrest me!" Nicole said in a near-shriek. "She just said she's not going to press charges."

"I'm not arresting you, but I am escorting you off-premises. And from now on, if I hear you've been anywhere near Ms. Davenport, the newspaper office, or the old funeral home, you will have to answer to the Foxfire Haven Constables."

Wow. He can be menacing when he wants to be.

Still, the stern demeanor seemed to be exactly what the situation needed. Without another glance at any of us, Nicole turned and stalked away as Wyatt easily kept pace next to her.

The gap Wyatt had left in our group was quickly filled by Sam, who rushed up, out of breath. "I was dealing with Aaron and that other guy. I'm so sorry, Jo. Are you okay?"

Except, Sam wasn't looking at Jo. He was gazing up at Barry with a slightly worried expression.

"I'm fine." Jo looked at Barry. "Thanks, Barry."

Barry's mouth moved, like he wanted to say something, but after a moment, his shoulders rounded, and he lowered his head. With a little nod, he turned and loped off through the crowd.

"I sure wasn't expecting this kind of drama tonight," Sam said. "You're really okay, Jo?"

"Yeah, Sam, I'm fine. Barry caught Nicole just as she lunged for me."

"Okay, well. All right. I'm going to get a drink. Why did I think this party was a good idea?" Sam wandered off in the direction of the bar.

Now that it was just our coven standing together, I reached out and took Jo's hand. "Is that the first time you've seen Barry since you two broke up?"

Jo started. Valerian looked mildly surprised, but Marlee barely flinched.

"How did you know?" Jo asked.

"Every time you come into the tavern, you're clearly looking around for someone."

"Am I that obvious?"

"Yes," the three of us chorused.

"Plus," I added, "when you were tearing up your old intentions the other morning, there was something about those little pieces of paper with your handwriting on them that reminded me of something. Seeing Barry standing here, with you, made me realize what it was. He hired me a while back to take some things from his house to a thrift store. One of the items was a beautiful desk chair, and there was a torn piece of paper wedged between the arm and the cushion. I didn't recognize the writing at the time, but it said something about a beautiful view."

"One of my intentions," Jo said. "Barry got me that chair so I could sometimes work from his place."

"Why didn't you ever tell us you and Barry dated?" Valerian asked. "I figured out a long time ago that he was drinking all that whiskey to nurse a broken heart, but I didn't realize it was you he was trying to get over."

Jo shrugged. "Our relationship was no secret, but he's a very private person. It's not easy for him, being the only Bigfoot in town. He doesn't like all the attention. So, when we broke up, it felt like not broadcasting it was the more polite thing to do."

I frowned. Barry seemed so nice, and I had been enjoying getting to know him better the few times we'd talked. But that version of Barry didn't match the image I had of Jo's ex-boyfriend. "He's the one who told you it was stupid to turn down that associate editor position in Vesta Falls?" I asked.

"Oh, no," Jo said quickly. "My family used that terminology. Barry never said that. But he was afraid that I was considering turning down the job just so I could stay here, with him. He said he didn't want to come between me and my career, so he broke up with me. He said it was better for me to follow my dreams."

"But then you turned down the job, anyway," I pointed out.

"Like I told Barry, I stayed because Foxfire Haven is my home, and I want my future to be with this newspaper. It was never about him. I mean, maybe it was a little bit, but, ultimately, I stayed because of my career goals."

Without a word, we all stepped toward Jo and squashed her in a giant group hug.

"I can feel it," Marlee said. "You were accused of murder, you were attacked, and you had a run-in with your ex, all in one night! Oh, our sweet Jo. I know it hurts."

"I'll be okay. I've got my coven." At least, I thought that was what Jo had said. Her face was buried in Valerian's shoulder, so it was hard to tell.

We broke the hug but remained standing in a tight circle.

"That money accusation was ridiculous," Jo said. "It's bad enough Nicole has it out for me, but I can't believe she tried to point the finger at our entire coven."

"I kind of feel bad for her," Marlee said. "If she was always following Wanda around, she might not have a lot of friends. And, now that Wanda is dead, she's all by herself in a strange town. Her accusing us of conspiring together might be more about jealousy than any real suspicion."

"Jealousy?" Valerian asked. "Are you saying she wishes she was the best bartender in Foxfire Haven?"

Marlee laughed. "I'm saying she probably wishes she had friends like us. Jo just said she's got her coven, and that's exactly it. We stand up for each other."

"With the help of a Bigfoot now and then," I pointed out.

"And a ghost who ensures we look great thanks to his fashion advice," Jo added.

The four of us laughed.

"I'm heading back to the bar," Valerian said. She gestured toward the still-full drinks she had brought over before Nicole had interrupted us. "Marlee needs to recover for a while longer yet, so you three stay here, enjoy your drinks, and try not to get into any more trouble."

"Trouble keeps finding us," Jo muttered.

For the next ten minutes, though, trouble kept its distance. A few people Jo and Marlee knew came over to say hello, and we did exactly as Valerian had instructed, sipping our drinks and enjoying some quiet conversation.

At one point, I turned to look around the room, and I saw that Aaron and Ilya were nowhere to be found. I doubted either of them had been arrested, but I figured they had, at least, been kicked out of the party.

"Wanda would have loved this, wouldn't she?" I said suddenly. "I mean, I didn't really know the woman, but she seems like the type who would have been delighted by all this drama. Her ex punched her P.I., and then her personal assistant accused Jo of murder and an entire coven of conspiracy. And it all happened because her death brought us here together today."

"She would have inserted herself right into the middle of it all, no doubt," Marlee said.

“Then let’s be grateful that her ghost didn’t stick around!” Jo pretended to shiver. “Can you imagine her ghost walking around here? The Phantom Foghorn of Foxfire Haven!”

I was still laughing when there was a gentle touch against my arm. Lenox Williams was standing there, looking gorgeous but also nervous. Her eyes flicked to Jo and Marlee, then back to me. “I think it’s time for me to come clean. Can we talk?”

Chapter Twenty-Five

"Why don't we go find somewhere quieter?" I suggested.

Lenox tilted her head toward the side of the room. "There's a quiet hallway back there. And I'd like all of you to come, please."

Jo, Marlee, and I exchanged curious glances as we followed Lenox down the hallway. The narrow space was deserted, and at the end, she turned into a room labeled *AV/Media*. It was filled with everything from CD players to an overhead projector. I was pretty sure I hadn't seen one of those in this millennium.

Marlee was the last person through the door, and she shut it behind her. The quiet felt blissful after the buzz of voices and music at the party.

"I'm going to take this information to the constables," Lenox began, "but they've got their hands full at the moment. And, considering the accusation against all of you, I want you to hear this from me."

"Was Nicole still accusing us as she was being escorted out?" Marlee asked. She looked both embarrassed and in awe of Nicole's audacity.

"She shouted it just before Chief Constable Hightower took her out."

"I'll be glad when she goes back to Florida," Jo said.

"Anyway," Lenox began. She stopped, blew out a breath, and laced her fingers tightly together. Then, in a rush, she said, "The bag of money was mine. It was a bribe to get Wanda to leave town."

Marlee, Jo, and I all had the exact same reaction, slapping a hand over our gaping mouths. It looked so comical that it coaxed a small smile onto Lenox's face, even though she was clearly nervous.

"Aaron was going to invest in the newspaper if she bought it," Lenox continued.

"And you felt betrayed by him," Marlee said, reaching a hand toward her. "I'm an empath, and I can feel how much it hurt you that Aaron would do that."

"She almost ruined me once before. Coming to Foxfire Haven was great for me, because I was able to start fresh. No one knew the financial disaster I'd gotten into back in Florida. It was good for Aaron to be here, too, because it was as far away as he could get from Wanda. She was so bad for him."

"He's mentioned his resentment of her," I said, "so I was also surprised when he told me Wanda had talked him into investing. She must have bullied him into a commitment."

"She sweet-talked him," Lenox said with a sneer. "He always said she could be nice when she wanted something, and he fell for it. That money he was going to give her was made from our business, and even though it's Aaron's share, and he can do whatever he wants with it, it would have been a risk."

"But the newspaper is in healthy shape. He should have made the money back," Jo said. She looked mildly offended at the insinuation that her employer ran a bad business.

"Oh, it's not that. Wanda would have found some reason why she needed more, and then more, and eventually, Aaron would be broke and scratching his head, wondering what had happened. I love that man like a brother, but he's really dumb when it comes to her."

"So, you wanted to bribe Wanda so she couldn't ruin Aaron." Marlee hitched up a shoulder. "It was a good plan, but clearly, something went wrong."

"It all went wrong when I handed her the bag of money." Lenox's eyes flashed, and she stared at a point on the wall as she recounted the experience. "She took the bag, then laughed right in my face. She told me she wasn't going anywhere, or giving the money back. And she threatened that if I told anyone, she would ruin me."

"By telling everyone in town what Ilya had learned about you in Florida," I finished.

"All of that makes sense," Marlee said. She suddenly swayed, and she grabbed my arm to steady herself. "Sorry. I'm still a bit weak from all the emotions of the night. Anyway, what *doesn't* make sense to me is that the money wound up stashed behind the trash bin in the alley."

"I don't know the how or why of that," Lenox said. "Wanda walked off with the cash like she was the queen of this town, and I went home and ate an entire pint of ice cream to make myself feel better. When I read the newspaper article about the money being found, I knew it was what I'd given Wanda, but for the life of me, I have no idea why it was hidden out behind the tavern."

"You gave Wanda a ton of money, and she laughed at you, then threatened you, then turned up dead." Jo was looking at Lenox with one eyebrow arched. "You know how bad that makes you look, right?"

"I know. It's why I've been too afraid to tell the constables the money came from me."

"I can feel your panic," Marlee said, "but I believe you're innocent."

"I hope the constables agree. And by telling them the truth, maybe it will make me seem less suspicious."

"There's an upside to this," I pointed out. "All that money is just sitting there at the station, because no one knows whose it is. If you're telling the truth, and you can prove it, then you'll get your money back."

"I can prove it. The cash withdrawal from my savings matches the amount of cash in that bag. And, if that's not enough, I was lucky in at least one thing: I met Wanda outside city hall."

Jo's face lit up in understanding. "Where they have security cameras!"

"Exactly. A look at the footage will show me handing the bag to Wanda."

Lenox looked slightly less scared since we had taken her confession with grace, and I hoped she would, in fact, get her money back. It sounded like her intentions had been good, though Jo made a fair point that the backfiring bribe only made Lenox look more like a suspect.

We thanked Lenox for sharing her story with us, and then we all filed out of the room. When we got back to the party, the buzz was definitely quieter than it had been. Things were beginning to wind down.

I was about to tell Marlee and Jo that I was going to head home for some much-needed sleep, when Lenox grabbed my arm. "Wait! Before you go. Aaron doesn't know about the bribe, so please don't tell him."

"We won't tell him," I assured her.

Lenox took off, and I turned to Jo and Marlee. "At least we're getting some answers," I said.

"But we still don't know how the money, which was in Wanda's possession at one time, wound up in the alley," Jo said.

"Lenox is trying to be helpful by coming clean, but now we just have more questions." I shook my head.

"Such as," Marlee said, "was Wanda murdered for the money? And if so, why didn't the killer take off with it? Or was Wanda killed for some other reason?"

"Not my concern at the moment," I declared. "I just want bed."

"But we'll stay and help you tear down this party," Jo told Marlee.

"We will?" I yawned. "Yeah, we will. Covens stick together."

The party might have been dying down, but the handful of people who remained were in no mood to give up their night of fun. It was eleven o'clock by the time the last few stragglers left, and then we treated tear-down like an Olympic sport.

I went to bed just after midnight, my back aching and my brain racing. Thankfully, neither one of those things kept me up for long.

All four of us slept in on Sunday morning. By the time I emerged into the kitchen, in desperate need of coffee, the others were already gathered around the breakfast table. All four of our familiars were in the kitchen, too, and Perkins stamped his tiny feet against the windowsill. Whether he was happy to see me or complaining about my lazy morning, I wasn't sure.

"Marlee," I said, "the next time someone dies in this town, please don't say yes to coordinating their party."

"I'm willing to compromise with you," Marlee said. I noticed she had dark circles under her eyes. It would probably take her days to recover from all the strong emotions that had assaulted her the night before. "I'll take any and every job that comes my way during my slow season. In my busy months, I'll stick to weddings, birthdays, and other fun things."

"I've been to weddings that were way more drama than last night's party," Valerian pointed out.

"What are we all doing today?" I asked as I slid into the vacant chair at the table.

"I'm going back to bed, and I'm taking a book plus a bag of chocolate chip cookies with me," Marlee said.

"I'm going to work at eleven, so I've got"—Valerian looked at her watch and made a noise of disgust—"not much time before I have to go."

"And I," Jo said, "am taking Gordon to the beach. He loves flying along the shoreline in winter."

"You should have told us," Marlee chastised. "We could have planned to go with you."

Jo shook her head. "Nope. This is something just Gordie and I do every January."

"Don't tell the other familiars," I said, eyeing Perkins. "They might get jealous."

"And you?" Valerian prompted. "What's your plan today?"

"I'm heading to the supermarket." I paused. "That's it. That's my day. And I'm very excited about it."

Soon, Marlee and I were the only ones still at home. She had disappeared into her room with not just a book and cookies, but a cup of tea and a plate of three cupcakes, too. The cupcakes were leftovers from the party the night before, and Marlee said she was sure Sam didn't want them, since he took home a dozen, and she would have felt bad throwing them out.

Then, Marlee had added, "If there had been four, I would have said each one of us gets a cupcake. But since there are only three, someone would have been left out. I didn't want to hurt anyone's feelings."

"So, you're doing the nice thing by eating them all yourself," I had replied with a laugh.

"Someone has to make the sacrifice."

Now, I pictured Marlee curled up in her bed like a cozy little spider, surrounded not by bugs but by treats. It would be exactly what she needed to help her continue recovering.

I headed for the supermarket before I could talk myself into a book and cookies, too. I went armed with a list of ingredients for a stew and a stir-fry, and I was steadily filling up my cart when I spotted Gnorris eyeing a display of very sugary cereal.

"Do gnomes like really sweet things?" I asked in greeting.

Gnorris turned, and I could see the excitement on his face. "Oh, yes. Almost as much as fairies do. And this new cereal looks extra sugary."

"By the way," I said, "I really am sorry about that whole debacle at the magical plant class Friday night."

Gnorris waved away my apology with one hand while his other reached for a box of the cereal. "I was looking forward to a boost in business from the gossip, but it turned out even better than that. That man Lenox yelled at, he came in to apologize. And, he ordered a massive flower arrangement. He dropped a ton of money on it, all just so he could cheer up his fiancée. It cheered me up, too!"

"Fiancée? But, I thought Ilya came to Foxfire Haven by himself? He's a private investigator who's done work for Wanda."

Gnorris didn't seem nearly as curious as me about Ilya's flower order. He shrugged, then chucked the cereal box into his cart. He was using one of the tiny ones that were made for kids to push around when they shopped with their parents. "He said something about his fiancée losing a bunch of money recently, and then they had a fight, and it was all his fault, so he wanted to cheer her up."

"Lost a bunch of...? But... Oh. We've been looking at this all wrong."

CHAPTER TWENTY-SIX

GNORRIS CHORTLED, BOTH HANDS pressed against his belly. The skin around his eyes crinkled as he said, "You just cracked the case!"

"Maybe, but I'm not sure. I have to go!"

I turned and took two strides toward the front of the store when Gnorris called, "But wait! Your groceries!"

Oh, right. I looked back at my cart. It would be rude to abandon it in the middle of the aisle, I thought. Besides, some of the things in it were for dinner that night. I wanted to solve a murder, but I also wanted a tasty chicken stir-fry.

With a frustrated sigh, I grabbed the cart, turned it around, and nearly ran to the checkout with the shortest line. Behind me, I distantly heard Gnorris call, "This is the second time I've helped you solve a murder. I must be your good-luck charm!"

I was out of breath as I threw items onto the belt at the checkout, and the person in line ahead of me gave me a concerned look.

"Sorry," I mumbled. I forced myself to move slower, and I tried to breathe in a more measured way, but I was too full of nervous energy to stand still. I grabbed a copy of *Magic Monthly*, the tacky tabloid for witches, then put it back. Next, I picked up and put back nearly every candy bar in the display rack.

Finally, it was my turn. As the cashier scanned my items, she kept glancing at me. "You're that witch," she said.

"Which one?"

"The one who drives a hearse."

"That's me."

"You look a little flushed. And your forehead is sweaty."

This lady would get along great with Holman.

"It's fine. I'm fine. Just in a bit of a hurry."

The woman didn't take the hint. If anything, her pace slowed as she looked more at me than at my groceries. "Is it true you found a dead body inside that hearse you drive around town?"

"Under. I found a body under the hearse, inside my garage." I started chucking the already-filled shopping bags into my cart.

Three items to go. Two. One.

Whew.

I paid, then took off. All I could think about was my new theory, and how anxious I was to tell Wyatt.

But, I remembered, *it's Sunday. He might not even be at the station.*

I reached the hearse, and as I began loading my groceries into the back with one hand, I pulled out my phone and called Wyatt with the other.

It went to voicemail, and I muttered a few words I would never want my mother to hear me saying. "I think I know who killed Wanda!" I nearly shouted into the phone after the recording of Wyatt's voice told me to leave a message. "Oh, it's Hazel. Where are you?"

"I'm right behind you."

I whirled around and saw Wyatt standing there, smirking at me. He was wearing a charcoal-gray wool coat with a maroon scarf. I would never admit how handsome he looked.

"I saw you heading to your car and thought I'd come over to ask if Ms. Davenport is doing all right after that scene last night."

"She's okay, thank you." I slammed the back of the hearse shut. "Wyatt, this murder wasn't about hurting Wanda, or getting revenge on her. It was about creating an opportunity!"

"An opportunity?"

"Yes! I mean, I think it was. Let me tell you my theory."

Wyatt lifted one finger. "Hold that thought." He pulled his phone out of his coat pocket, and I could hear the buzz as it vibrated.

Whomever was calling him had the worst timing ever.

Wyatt listened for a moment, then said, "We'll be right there," and hung up.

"We?" I asked.

"Yes. I want to know your theory about Wanda's killer, and I suspect that what we'll find at the tavern will tell you whether or not you're on the right track."

"But my groceries..."

Wyatt just raised an eyebrow, and I knew it was his way of asking, *Do you want to solve a murder, or do you want to keep your chicken from going bad?*

"Okay, but I'm going to follow you in the hearse, and I can throw the cold stuff into the fridge at the tavern."

"Drive fast," Wyatt said, already turning to head for the squad car that was parked nearby. "But don't break the speed limit!"

Wyatt, I was pretty sure, broke the speed limit before he even left the parking lot. I didn't know what was happening at the tavern, but I did know he wanted to get there quickly.

I followed at a much slower pace. There was no way I was going to treat the hearse like a sports car. I parked on the curb outside the tavern, ran to the back of the hearse to grab the bags of chicken and other items that needed to be kept cold, and headed inside.

I forgot about the grocery bags in my hands as soon as I saw the scene in front of me. Wyatt and three other constables had clearly just broken up a fight. A table and three chairs had been overturned, and several drinks had fallen to the wooden floor, sending liquid and shards of glass everywhere.

On one side of the mess, two constables were restraining Aaron and Lenox, who both looked disheveled. Aaron had a growing red stain on his white sweatshirt. At first, I worried it was blood, but it was too pale. Wine, probably.

On the other side, Wyatt and another constable had both Ilya and Nicole held by the upper arms. Nicole's lipstick was smeared across one cheek, and when Ilya bared his teeth, I could see he had a chipped tooth.

"What started all of this?" Wyatt asked, his tone even.

Aaron, Lenox, Ilya, and Nicole all began shouting at once, and Wyatt roared for them to be quiet.

In the silence that followed, I said quietly, "I think I can answer that."

Every head in the tavern turned toward me, and I felt the same way I had in the tenth grade, when I'd had to give a speech in front of the whole school. I wanted to shrink back into the shadows, but it was too late to hide now.

"Nicole wanted to be a journalist," I said as I set my bags down on a nearby table. "That was her dream, but Wanda made her be a personal assistant, instead, catering to her every whim. Many years ago, Wanda nearly ruined Lenox's career goals, too. When Wanda showed up in Foxfire Haven, Lenox tried to bribe her with a bag full of cash to leave town, so she and Aaron wouldn't have to deal with her again."

Lenox is going to be unhappy that I spilled the beans to the whole tavern about that, I thought. But, it was too late now, so I continued. "That money represented a huge financial opportunity. If Wanda was out of the way, Nicole would be free to pursue the career she wanted, and she would have all that money to help her as she started a new life."

The color drained from Nicole's face, but her expression was still angry. "I did not kill Wanda!"

"No one had counted on a coven of witches stumbling on the cash before it could be moved to a safe location. I heard Nicole and Sam arguing at the party last night. Nicole wanted to buy the newspaper since Wanda couldn't, but she told Sam it didn't matter that he wouldn't sell to her since she didn't have the money anymore, anyway."

I met Nicole's eyes. "It was the 'anymore' that stood out. You were going to use the cash to buy the newspaper. Then, you could be not just a journalist, but an editor and publisher, too. Wanda's death and that money of hers cleared every roadblock for you. Except, we found the cash and turned it in to the constables, and in your anger, you accused us of conspiring to kill Wanda."

"But I didn't kill her." Nicole was starting to cry, and her voice was thick.

"Did you like the flowers your fiancé gave you? Ilya told Gnorris the two of you had a fight, and that you'd lost a lot of money, so he wanted to give you some flowers to make you feel better. He also killed Wanda to make things better for you."

Nicole turned to Ilya, and she shook her head, almost imperceptibly. "No," she whispered.

"I expect you already figured that part out, though," I said. "Ilya didn't come to Foxfire Haven because he was working for Wanda. He came here for you. Except, you told me Wanda wouldn't even allow you to date, so the two of you had to keep your relationship a secret. Ilya knew that if he ran into Wanda here, he could claim he'd come to town to help her out."

In answer, Nicole just dropped her head.

"When I saw the two of you at the park, shortly after Wanda's murder, I should have realized then that you two knew each other, but I told myself Ilya was just a friendly stranger offering his condolences. You could have gone to Ilya the night Wanda went missing, but you came to my house, instead, because you were supposed to be acting like you were all alone in town."

"Every time Nicole would try to resign or ask for a job where she could write, Wanda would threaten to ruin her reputation." Ilya sounded indignant. "I was hoping to dig up something bad about Wanda, so we could turn the threats on her. If I could blackmail her, she'd have to let Nicole go or risk being ruined."

"And the added bonus of all that money was too much for you to resist, wasn't it?" Wyatt asked. He still had one of Ilya's arms in his grip, and he looked thoroughly disgusted. "You skipped blackmail and went right to murder."

"I was tailing Wanda, and I saw Lenox give her all that money. So, I lied and told Wanda I'd found information about Sam that she could use against him, forcing him to sell the newspaper for a lower price. I told Wanda I expected to be paid well for my services, she agreed, and then I said I would handle setting up a meeting with Sam at the newspaper office one night. That way, we could get the deal done quietly, when no one else was there."

"Except it was just you and Wanda who were there that night," I guessed.

"Of course. The lock on that old door was easy to pick. After she'd been taken care of, I just needed to get the money. Nicole had a key to Wanda's hotel room, so I used it to get the bag of cash. But, I figured I might become a suspect in Wanda's death, and if the constables searched my room, they would find it. So, I stashed it out behind this place. I never thought someone would discover the money before I could find a better hiding spot for it."

Nicole was crying harder. "You told me you just took the money. You didn't tell me you... You said you weren't the one who..."

"I did it for you!" Ilya cried. He looked utterly confused that Nicole was horrified by his confession. "She was ruining your life!"

When Ilya tried to reach his free arm toward Nicole, she shook her head wildly. She stepped away with so much force that the constable holding onto her nearly lost her grip on Nicole's arm.

"Nicole, please. I love you!" Ilya didn't even seem to notice that Wyatt was reading him his rights and putting him in handcuffs. All he could see was Nicole.

"Wild," said a voice over my left shoulder.

I turned to see Jo standing just behind me, and I couldn't help the quiet chuckle that escaped my lips. She had her notebook out, and she was furiously writing down details for what I knew would be a front-page story in the newspaper.

Chapter Twenty-Seven

"To Jo's future as editor and publisher of the *Foxfire Haven Recorder*!" Marlee had a wide smile on her face as she clinked her glass against each of ours.

After we had all taken a sip of the new cocktail recipe Valerian was testing out on her coven, Jo said, "Thank you, but I'd like to point out this is the second toast we've done to me and my career."

"We can toast someone else, then," I said. I had put my glass down on the table in the breakfast nook, but I lifted it once again. "To Marlee, for pulling off a most memorable party at the last minute!"

After that, Jo lifted her glass. "To Val, who raked in tips at the tavern after the arrest!"

"I'll take more drama any day, if it means big tips!" Valerian said. "And here's to Hazel for solving the murder!"

It had been three days since the showdown at the tavern, as Valerian had taken to calling it. Already, town gossip was turning the whole event into something much more dramatic. I'd heard several different versions of the story from people who weren't there, including one that involved Lenox standing on a table and launching herself at Nicole, like something from a professional wrestling match. I'd also heard one rumor about Aaron trying to hex Ilya.

According to Valerian, who had witnessed the whole thing from her spot behind the bar, it hadn't been that dramatic. Ilya and Nicole had been sitting at a table, having a drink. When Aaron and Lenox walked into the tavern, Aaron got angry all over again and lunged at Ilya. Worried about getting punched in the face for the second time in two days, Ilya had jumped up and out of the way so quickly that he'd overturned the table and chairs. In the process, he had tripped and fallen. On his way to the ground, Ilya had accidentally hit Nicole's face with one flailing hand, smearing her lipstick. He had also chipped his tooth on the edge of a chair.

Lots of shouting and finger-pointing had ensued, and two constables who were walking past on the sidewalk out front had heard the commotion. They had broken up the fight before it could get past a bit of shoving, and the only real damage done had been to Ilya's tooth, which was, ultimately, his own fault.

"It's a shame the constables didn't give you all that money as a reward for figuring out that Ilya was the killer," Jo said wistfully.

I took a long sip of my drink, then sighed dramatically. "It is a shame. But, honestly, I'm happy Lenox was able to get her money back."

I was also happy the past few days had been nice and quiet. I'd had another video call with my granddaughter, Hailey, and I'd had my usual slew of clients to make deliveries for. It wasn't hectic, but it was steady, unlike the chaos of helping Marlee prep for the party.

Even our familiars were celebrating our successes. Gordon was on the kitchen counter, with Lonnie at his side. Stella and Perkins were both on the windowsill.

Outside, it was cold and rainy and dark, but inside, everything was bright and cozy.

Even as I was looking around the kitchen and appreciating how good we were all feeling, a can of green beans sailed from its spot on the counter to the far wall, where it smacked the wainscoting with a loud crash, then clattered to the floor.

We all stared silently at the can as it slowly rolled to a stop.

"There *is* a ghost here who's not Holman," Marlee said. "I'd really hoped my laundry flying across the room was just gravity, or maybe a tiny earthquake, and not the work of a poltergeist."

I swallowed hard. "It's like Barry said. Us being here is waking it up."

"I talked to him today," Jo said.

"The ghost?" Marlee asked incredulously.

"No! Barry. It was awkward, but it also felt really good. He said he understands I wanted to stay in Foxfire Haven for reasons that had nothing to do with him."

"Does this mean you two are getting back together?" I asked.

"No, but now I can move on a bit easier."

"And stop looking for him every time you come into the tavern?" Valerian was looking at Jo skeptically.

"Well, I don't know about that." Jo cleared her throat. "Anyway, back to this ghost we've awakened."

She's not over him yet. I reached out and briefly put my hand over Jo's, giving it a reassuring squeeze.

Then, I said, "I want to know how much Uncle Grant knew about this other ghost. He must have noticed the dark-haired ghost that we saw in that one old photo."

"We still don't know if that ghost and the one chucking things across the room are one and the same," Marlee pointed out.

"What I want to know is if my collection of glass roses is in danger!" Valerian was looking around the room defiantly.

"As our magic grows, so will the entity's power," I said as I also gazed around the kitchen. "I think we need to be ready for anything."

A NOTE FROM THE AUTHOR

Sometimes, I think the character I relate to the most is Jo, the manifesting witch whose written words become reality. I wrote my Eternal Rest Bed and Breakfast series about a haunted Victorian house, and then I wound up living in a haunted Victorian house. Except, like Jo, it wasn't quite what I'd envisioned. Instead of a stately Queen Anne mansion in North Georgia, I got a bungalow in Arizona. Coincidence or magic? Maybe that's part of the joy of writing paranormal cozy mysteries: no matter how wild the stories get, they still manage to reflect real life. Thank you for reading, and may you also find the magic in your life.

While Jo is writing intentions, will you please write a review? It helps enormously. Thank you!

Eternally Yours,

Beth

P.S. You can keep up with my latest book news, get fun

freebies, and more by signing up for my newsletter at BethDolgner.com!

Next in Series

Find out what's next for Hazel and the Crones of a Feather!

Crystals and Conspiracies
Crones of a Feather Paranormal Cozy Mysteries Book 4

An accused vampire, a disgruntled witch, and dark sorcery. At this magic shop, death has no expiration date.

Hazel Underwood and Adeline Beaumont do not get along. But the vampire who runs the local magic store will have to put her trust in Hazel when someone is murdered in the store, and Adeline is blamed for it.

A vengeful customer might have framed Adeline, but Hazel begins to hear whispers of something much more sinister happening in the small magical town. Is there dark magic at work in Foxfire Haven, Washington?

It will take the combined efforts of Hazel and her coven to uncover the truth and clear Adeline's name. At the same time, Hazel is on the brink of losing control of her magic as paranormal activity at home gets dangerous...

ACKNOWLEDGMENTS

As always, I am grateful for the team of people who help me publish a book. My test readers, my ARC team, and my editors are invaluable in helping me refine each manuscript. I am also grateful to you, dear reader, for being with me on this adventure. Thank you.

BOOKS BY BETH DOLGNER

Crones of a Feather
Paranormal Cozy Mystery Series
Spells and Subterfuge
Divination and Deceit
Manifesting and Mischief
Crystals and Conspiracies

Nightmare, Arizona
Paranormal Cozy Mystery Series
Homicide at the Haunted House
Drowning at the Diner
Slaying at the Saloon
Murder at the Motel
Poisoning at the Party
Headless at Halloween (Novella)
Clawing at the Corral
Axing at the Antique Store
Fatality at the Festival
Terminated at the Trailhead
Body at the Bakery

Eternal Rest Bed and Breakfast

Paranormal Cozy Mystery Series
Sweet Dreams
Late Checkout
Picture Perfect
Destination Wedding (Novella)
Scenic Views
Breakfast Included
Groups Welcome
Quiet Nights
Halloween Vibes (Novella)

Betty Boo, Ghost Hunter
Romantic Urban Fantasy Series
Ghost of a Threat
Ghost of a Whisper
Ghost of a Memory
Ghost of a Hope

Manifest
Young Adult Steampunk

A Talent for Death
Young Adult Urban Fantasy

Non-fiction
Georgia Spirits and Specters
Everyday Voodoo

ABOUT THE AUTHOR

Beth Dolgner's career as an author began in nonfiction with *Georgia Spirits and Specters*, a collection of Georgia ghost stories. From there, Beth entered the world of ghost hunting and was a longtime guide with the Roswell Ghost Tour in Georgia. She also lectures on Victorian death and mourning customs as well as Victorian Spiritualism, which stemmed from her volunteer work with Atlanta's Historic Oakland Cemetery. Beth likes to think of it all as research for her books.

Outside of writing, Beth enjoys traveling, sewing, and trying to convince her husband, Ed, that ghosts are real.

Keep up with Beth and sign up for her newsletter at BethDolgner.com.

www.ingramcontent.com/pod-product-compliance
Lightning Source LLC
LaVergne TN
LVHW091133080826
845145LV00008B/2138

* 9 7 8 1 9 5 8 5 8 7 4 5 4 *